Jo whacked, and quite right, people didn't have to be fat. If Lol weren't fat she might feel better about herself and then she wouldn't be the pain that she was; but she *was* fat and she *was* a pain, and it was entirely her own fault, so why should Jo worry about her? She would tell Barge, first thing Monday morning, that she was joining the Gang and Lol could go and – go and *stuff* herself.

By the same author:

You-Two
A Bottled Cherry Angel
Frankie's Dad

Fat Lollipop

Jean Ure

RED FOX

A Red Fox Book
Published by Random House Children's Books
20 Vauxhall Bridge Road, London SW1V 2SA

A division of the Random House Group
London Melbourne Sydney Auckland
Johannesburg and agencies throughout the world

First published by Hutchinson Children's Books 1991

Red Fox edition 1992

Printed and bound in Great Britain by
Cox & Wyman Ltd, Reading, Berkshire

ISBN 0 09 997740 0

FAT LOLLIPOP

1

'Bozzy, Jammy, Fij and Barge. You must admit,' said
Barge, 'it does *sound* better.'

'Heaps better than Bozzy, *Lol*, Fij and Barge.'

'Which doesn't scan,' said Fij.

'You have to admit,' urged Barge.

They looked across at Joanne Jameson, known to her
friends as Jammy (to her family as Jo). They were all four
perched somewhat uncomfortably on upturned flower
pots in one of the gardening sheds, where in fact they had
no right to be but as Barge had said, 'It's the only place one
can be private for five minutes.' By private she meant away
from Laurel Bustamente (otherwise known as Lol).

'Bozzy, Jammy, Fij and Barge . . .'

Short bouncy Bozzy, with her stubby blond plaits and
bulgy blue eyes; medium-sized Jo – 'Jo in the middle', as
she had been called at Juniors; long willowy Fij and big,
bossy, square-shouldered Barge.

'It *goes*,' said Bozzy.

'Like a poem,' said Barge, waxing rhapsodical.

'Or at any rate,' said Fij, 'a bit of doggerel.'

'*You* may think of it as doggerel: to me it sounds like a
poem . . . Beauty,' said Barge, 'is in the ear of the
beholder.'

'Oh! Quite. But I thought we were talking of Jam
becoming one of us?'

1

They looked again at Jo.

'It has a definite ring to it,' said Barge, 'I think you will agree.'

Jo was only too happy to agree – she would be only too happy to become one of them. The Laing Gang (Margery Laing, Chloë Boswood, and Felicity Isobel Jarvis) were a force to be reckoned with in Class 1N. They had all been at Petersham & St Mary's since the Infants, moving up together through the school, from the Elms to the Homestead to number ninety-four, which was where the senior school was housed. People such as Jo, transferring from other, inferior establishments (by definition, all other establishments were inferior to Peter's) could only be regarded as Lesser Beings, at any rate to begin with. For a Lesser Being to be courted by a gang of ex-Homesteaders was almost unheard of.

The Laing Gang had, in fact, first approached Jo last term, the Christmas term, when she had been exceedingly new indeed, but last term there had been Matty. Jo and Matty had been best friends since their early days at Juniors; there could be no question of one of them joining a gang without the other. But that had been last term, and things had changed since then. Jo and Matty were still friends, only Matty, now, was going round with Julie-Ann Gillon, while Jo wasn't going round with anyone. She had tried making friends with Claire Kramer, but it wasn't really possible to make friends with someone as single-minded as Claire. She had only one thought in her head, and that was ballet; there simply wasn't room for anything else. It left Jo pretty much out in the cold.

2

'*So*,' said Barge, in her meaningful, Bargelike way.

They all sat there, on their flower pots, looking expectantly at Jo. It would be so easy – all she had to do was say yes. The prospect of a whole term on her own was not much fun, and if she didn't join the Laing Gang who else was there? There was Nadge, but Nadge was far too much in demand to be bothered with a nonentity, and besides she had all her old mates from the Homestead. Admittedly, they were in different houses, and on the whole it wasn't done to have friends in a house other than your own, but Nadge was a law unto herself. She did just whatever she wanted, and because she was Nadge, and brilliant at games, and probably the most popular person in the whole of the first year, no one ever said anything.

Then there was the Stubbs Gang – Gerry Stubbs, Pru Frank and Naomi Adams – but they were just too clever for words; they wouldn't want an ignoramus like Jo lowering their standards. And the Bookends (Sally Hutchins and Emma Gilmore) were self-sufficient, and she certainly wasn't going to tag along being odd-man-out with Matty and Jool. That only left Melanie Peach and Ashley Wilkerson.

Melanie was all right, except for being a bit over-theatrical (she had an uncle who was a TV star, a fact which no one was ever allowed to forget). Ashley – well, Ashley wasn't anything, really. An almost total nonentity. She had attached herself to Melanie for want of anyone else to attach herself to and now drifted along behind her like a pale, worshipful shadow. Jo suspected that a shadow was all Melanie wanted. She would probably be quite happy to have Jo in attendance as

3

well, but then Ashley would be put out and anyway Jo didn't really think that she wanted to be a shadow, whereas she had felt for a long time that she would like to be friends with Fij. Barge had a tendency to throw her weight around, and Bozzy, though small, could be extraordinarily belligerent; it was Fij, tall skinny Fij, with her droopy face and long mousy hair, who was the voice of moderation. Even Matty agreed that Fij was 'really nice'.

'You see, I do *feel*,' said Barge, 'that with Jam as number four we could be the Gang we used to be, back in the Homestead.'

'Before Mo left to go to Heathfield.'

It was tremendously flattering. Jo knew all about the wonderful Mo, and how absolutely irreplaceable she had been. She leant forward, a trifle perilously on her upturned flower pot, intending to say, 'All right! I'll join!' when instead, to her immense indignation, she heard a voice which presumably had to be hers, since she couldn't see anyone else's lips moving, pipe up with: 'What about Lol?'

'Oh! Fiddle faddle to Lol!' Barge made an expansive gesture and fell off her flower pot. Picking herself up she said, 'You don't want to worry about old Fat Lollipop.'

'Fat Lollipop,' said Bozzy, 'is a fat pain.'

'Yes, but –' Jo's voice spoke again: she did wish it would shut up – 'I suppose she can't *help* it.'

'Yes, she can. She eats too much.'

'And anyway, it isn't just that.' Fij, as always, strove to be fair. 'One doesn't object to people being podgy, so long as they are *nice* podgy. But Lol is so –' She waved a hand.

4

'*Irritating*,' said Bozzy.

'Always *knows* everything.' (That was a bit rich, coming from Barge: Barge knew more about everything than almost anybody.)

'Always *got* everything –'

'Always *done* everything –'

'Always *been* everywhere.'

'Besides,' said Fij, 'she was never properly one of us. Not really.'

'That's right.' Barge nodded. 'She just shoved her way in.'

'So it's entirely her own fault,' said Bozzy, 'if we now shove her back out again.'

'But won't she be upset?' said Jo.

'Probably.' Barge humped a shoulder. 'But one can't go through life not doing things just because it might upset someone. I mean, Stanny was obviously upset when I copied out my maths homework from Bozzy the other day, but that didn't stop me doing it.'

'No, and it didn't stop Stanny giving you a dose of double homework,' pointed out Fij.

'If you're implying that Fat Lollipop will take some mean and beastly form of revenge –' Barge huffed, self-importantly. 'I think we're quite capable of dealing with *her*, thank you very much.'

'Have you spoken to her about it?' said Jo.

'Not yet.' said Bozzy. 'We thought we'd talk to you first.'

'It makes me feel so awful,' said Jo. 'Like a – a usurper, or something.'

Bozzy pulled one of her stubby blond plaits as near to her mouth as it would reach and did her best to chew on it. She considered Jo, wonderingly, out of bulging blue eyes. It was possible she didn't know what the word usurper meant: English was not Bozzy's strongest subject. (In fact Bozzy didn't really have a strongest subject, she managed to do equally badly in them all. Only last week Miss Lloyd, their form mistress, had said, 'Well, Chloë, at least you are consistent, I'll say that for you!')

'Like in History,' said Jo. 'When Bolingbroke went and pushed Richard III off the throne and called himself Henry IV.'

'Well, he could hardly call himself *Richard* IV,' said Bozzy, 'could he? Not if it wasn't his name.'

Bozzy had a positive genius for missing the point.

'I shouldn't worry yourself too much if I were you,' said Fij, comfortingly. 'After all, they were royalty.'

'Yes, and furthermore,' said Barge, 'Richard III was foully done in. All we're saying to Lol is, kindly run away and play with someone else, 'cause we're sick of you.'

Jo bit her lip. 'I suppose –' She hesitated.

'What?' said Fij.

'I suppose you couldn't possibly stretch the numbers to five?'

'No. You asked us that last term when you wanted Matty to join. We told you,' said Barge, 'we've *never* been five.'

'Five wouldn't be right,' said Fij. 'There'd always be an odd one.'

'Yes.' Jo sighed. 'I can see that.'

'So what –' Bozzy flung her arms wide, addressing the question to an invisible audience of thousands – 'what is the problem? Exactly?'

The problem was Lol; poor fat Lol. There wasn't anything malicious about Lol, it was just that she got on people's nerves. Jo couldn't help remembering last term when Miss Lloyd had set up the Christmas posting box and every single person except Lol had received great stackfuls of cards: Lol had only received three. Jo had felt bad about it even at the time. She had felt, even then, that she ought to have sent her one. Yet here she was, calmly proposing to get Lol thrown out of the Gang just so that she could take her place. Well, not quite *calmly*, perhaps. What she desperately wanted to say was, 'Problem? What problem?' and just forget all about it. If it didn't bother the others, why should it bother her?

She was on the point of clearing her throat to say precisely that when the door of the shed was pushed open and a head peered round. The head belonged to Michelle Wandres, a particularly unpleasant specimen of prefect.

'I thought I heard voices! What are you lot doing in here? You're not gardeners!' She glared at them. 'Are you?'

'In the Homestead,' volunteered Fij, 'I once planted an orange pip in a pot and it grew.'

'An *orange* pip!' marvelled Barge.

'In a *pot*,' enthused Bozzy.

'And it *grew*!'

Michelle was not impressed.

'You could have planted a giant redwood tree for all I care. It may have escaped your attention, but you are now in the Upper School and as you *very well know* these sheds are reserved solely for the use of gardeners. So scram, unless you want an order mark!'

They scrammed. As they did so, Barge hissed in Jo's ear, 'We'll give you till first thing Monday morning . . . not a minute longer!'

That afternoon, which was Friday, 1N had a hockey lesson which they shared with their rivals, 1Y. ('N' stood for Nelligan and 'Y' stood for York, two of the school houses, the other two being Sutton's and Roper's.) It was only the second Friday of term, and only their second hockey lesson, since last term they had played netball. They were still at the stage of practising passing before being allowed on to the hockey pitch for a real game.

Jo's heart sank when Miss Dysart told them to 'Choose partners! Hurry up! Let's get started.' At Juniors she had always been in demand; here at Peter's it was a question of teaming up with whoever was left over – which in this case happened to be Naomi. Nadge had gone with her best mate, Lee Powell, who was in York, Claire had brought a note from home which got her off hockey altogether (she was scared of hurting her ankles and ruining her future as a dancer), Matty was with Jool, Fij – pulling anguished faces at Jo – had been grabbed by Lol.

Stuck with Naomi, Jo couldn't help feeling a bit resentful. Not against Naomi, who after all couldn't help being clumsy and awkward and totally useless, but against Miss Dysart. Surely she could *see* that Jo wasn't able to get any proper practice? Fij couldn't, either. Lol had grown so enormous over the holidays that instead of running she could now only waddle. She had been quite fat last term, but this term she was positively huge. She must have spent the whole of Christmas glutting herself

8

on Christmas pudding and mince pies and pots and pots of double cream. If Jo and Fij could have been together they would have been passing up and down the field by now, like Lee and Nadge. (If Lol hadn't still been officially part of the Laing Gang, Jo and Fij *would* have been together.)

Jo whacked, crossly, at the ball. Bozzy was quite right, people didn't have to be fat. If Lol weren't fat she might feel better about herself and then she wouldn't be the pain that she was; but she *was* fat and she *was* a pain, and it was entirely her own fault, so why should Jo worry about her? She would tell Barge, first thing Monday morning, that she was joining the Gang and Lol could go and – go and *stuff* herself.

'Jo!' Miss Dysart cried out in warning as Jo slashed, viciously, at a stray ball. 'Do remember that hockey is supposed to be a game . . . not a battle!'

2

Next morning at breakfast, puddling with her spoon in her bowl of muesli, Jo said: 'You know when people get fat?'

'Get fat?' said Andy. 'You're hopeful!'

Tom guffawed. Both of Jo's brothers – Andy at sixteen, Tom at thirteen – were what Jo's mum called 'beefy'. Jo was the titchy one of the family. They thought it a great joke that she should talk of getting fat.

Patiently, Jo carved canals through the middle of her muesli. She was used to Andy teasing her and Tom being stupid.

'I didn't mean *me*. I meant other people.'

'I shouldn't think you did mean you!' Her mother leaned across and tapped her on the wrist. 'Just get on and get that down you and stop playing with it.'

'I don't like it,' said Jo.

'You liked it yesterday!'

'Yes, well, I don't like it now. It tastes funny. It's got dried fruit in it . . . ugh!' Jo pushed her plate away. 'I hate dried fruit!'

'I have never,' said Mrs Jameson, 'known such a faddy eater.'

'I'm not faddy! There's things I like and things I don't like . . . you *know* I don't like dried fruit.'

'So what are you going to eat?'

'I'll have an apple.'

'Apples are full of fungicides,' said Tom.

'Oh, for goodness' sake!' Mrs Jameson flapped at him, with the tea-cosy. 'Don't go putting her off one of the few things I can still get down her!'

'You can get nuts down me,' said Jo. 'S'long as they're not Brazil nuts. And *fresh* fruit. And chips, and chocolate.'

She helped herself to an apple from a bowl on the kitchen cabinet. If her father had been there he might have tried to make her eat the muesli, he was stricter than her mother, but on Saturdays he ran an antiques stall down the market and had to leave home at six o'clock. Jo's mum said that where Jo and her eating were concerned she had simply given up. It wasn't quite true, she did sometimes nag, but mostly she just let Jo eat what she wanted to eat, so that when the rest of the family were tucking into their meat and two veg., Jo was allowed to have just veg., or a handful of nuts and a banana – 'Like a monkey,' said Tom, who thought Jo ought to be stood over with a big stick as they were at school (at any rate, according to Tom. According to Tom they had a master at his school who knocked boys senseless if they didn't eat what they were given).

'Anyway,' said Jo, 'what I was saying . . . about people who get fat. Do you think they can help getting fat?'

'Yes,' said Andy. 'They eat too much and don't get enough exercise.'

'Unless it's glands,' said Mrs Jameson.

'Glands is a myth,' said Andy.

'That's a rather sweeping statement!'

11

'So what happens?' said Jo. 'If it's glands? What do people do?'

'Go to the doctor, I should think.'

Jo wondered if Lol had been to the doctor, or whether in Lol's case glands was a myth and it was just a case of gluttonising. She could see that it must be very difficult, for people who enjoyed things like Christmas pudding and Christmas cake and mince pies. Jo couldn't stand them. For dinner on Christmas Day she had just eaten vegetables with tinned peaches to follow.

'It's only women that are fat,' said Tom. 'Usually.'

'I resent that!' said Mrs Jameson. 'You can take that back, you sexist little brute!'

'I bet if you took all the girls in her school –' Tom pointed with his spoon at Jo – 'I bet there'd be more fat girls than we've got fat boys.'

'I bet there wouldn't, ' said Jo.

'I bet there would!'

'We've only got one fat girl in the whole of our year.'

'Well, we haven't got any, so there!'

'There is that boy in the fourth year,' said Andy. 'He's pretty vast.'

'Are people friends with him?' said Jo.

'Yes, he's quite popular. He played Falstaff last term in *Henry IV*.'

Lol, last term, had played one of the fairies in *A Midsummer Night's Dream*. Lots of people from 1N had been fairies – funny fairies. It had been a bit of a joke. Melanie had made herself a pair of orange peel teeth and Barge had gone clumping on in a pair of hockey boots. Fij had borrowed her mum's old glasses (without the lenses) and waved a broken wand, Jo had had a tiara

12

which kept falling down over her eyes. Lol had joined in with the rest of them. She had worn thick knee-length socks instead of tights, with a label prominently displayed on the back of her dress – SALE ITEM: Half Price. She hadn't seemed to mind making a laughing stock of herself. Jo wasn't sure that she would want to, if she were Lol's size.

'Anyhow, why?' said Mrs Jameson. 'Why do you want to know about being fat?' She looked at Jo, suspiciously. 'You're not getting anorexic, I hope?'

'I told you,' said Jo. 'It's somebody else.'

'Famous last words . . . ' said Andy.

When Jo went to bed that night she was almost certain that she had made up her mind: she was going to be a member of the Laing Gang and if Lol had to be chucked out that was just too bad. When all was said and done, Lol *had* pushed her way in; the others had never really wanted her. It was only that she had been in the Homestead with them and took it as her right, once Mo had gone. But it wasn't her right, you had to fit in to be part of a gang, and Lol didn't fit and never had fitted. It was Jo they had wanted all along and first thing on Monday she was going to go to Barge and say yes.

When she woke up on Sunday morning she found herself dithering all over again . . . Jo might be out in the cold but it was only due to circumstance, not because people didn't like her. Why, she had almost been voted vice games captain (Nadge, of course, was captain). Fij had beaten her by only one vote. *And* she was in the special gym team, and last term she had been in the House Under-13s netball team, and she was almost bound to get into the Under-13 rounders next term. Lol wasn't in anything, except the Laing Gang. They wouldn't chuck her out if Jo said no; they had to be four, and there wasn't anyone else.

After breakfast Matty came round. She lived next door, so out of school she and Jo still saw each other. They went up to Jo's bedroom, where they could talk without silly interruptions from Tom.

'Barge wants me to join her gang,' said Jo.

'Are you going to?'

'Dunno . . . can't make my mind up.'

'I think you ought,' said Matty.

Jo had never told Matty about her previous invitation to join the Laing Gang, but she could guess that Matty was feeling twinges of guilt on account of her having Jool and Jo not having anyone. Jo would have felt twinges of guilt had she been the one to make friends with someone else. She knew that you couldn't lay down rules: you couldn't *choose* who you were going to become friends with, any more than people could choose who they were going to fall in love with; but for some time she had felt hurt and betrayed. She didn't any more – well, only just now and again – but she could see that it would make it easier for Matty if she were to join forces with Barge & Co. It would stop the guilt feeling.

'Fij is nice,' said Matty.

'Yes; I know.'

'So what's stopping you? It's not that Claire, is it? You haven't still got a thing about her?'

Jo's cheeks grew slowly scarlet. 'I never had a thing about her!'

Matty was kind enough not to insist. (Jo, last term,

14

had behaved rather like a doormat where Claire was concerned.)

'It's nothing to do with her . . . it's Lol.'

'That fat thing!'

'If I join they'll chuck her out.'

'So what?'

'Well –' Jo picked at a hole in her duvet cover. 'It doesn't seem fair.'

'Don't see why. Gangs change all the time. It's not life membership, is it?'

'N-no, but – everyone's always so horrid to her!'

'Not surprised,' said Matty. 'Looking like she does . . . great blubber bag! It's enough to turn anyone off. She's so fat I can't hardly bear to look at her. When we're changing for gym or anything I just have to look the other way, else I'd be sick.'

It was all right for Matty, she was one of the tall lanky ones. She could eat like an elephant and never put on so much as an ounce.

Jo said, 'That's being fattist! It'd be like me saying I couldn't bear to look at you 'cause you're black or you saying you couldn't bear to look at me 'cause I'm white.'

'No, it wouldn't,' said Matty. 'Nothing wrong with being black or white. Being fat's revolting.'

'But if it's something she can't help –'

'Course she can help it!' Matty didn't believe in making excuses for people. 'You've seen her, stuffing her mouth . . . anyone'd be fat, they ate as much as she does.'

It was true, Jo had seen Lol, in the canteen at lunch time, waddling past with her tray piled high with fish and chips and sticky puddings.

She hardened her heart. She had turned down one opportunity to join the Gang, she wasn't turning down another. Lol would just have to take her chance.

3

On Monday morning, on their way in to school, who should Jo and Matty bump into but the Lollipop herself. It was really most unfortunate: Big Lol was the one person, on that day of all days, that Jo would far rather *not* have bumped into. What made it even worse was that Lol was in a confiding mood. First she confided, in cosy terms, that she had a boil on her bottom ('Who wants to *know* about it?' said Matty, afterwards), next she confided that when it was her birthday, which fortunately wasn't until after Easter, she was going to invite both Jo and Matty to her birthday party.

'I'm not going to invite everyone. I could if I wanted. Mum says I could invite the whole of our year, if I wanted. But I'm only going to have people I really like.'

Jo felt terrible. She thought, 'I can't bear it! It's like a nightmare.' She knew now how traitors must feel, pretending to make friends with people just so they could go and give them away to the enemy. And then she became aware that Lol had stopped talking and that Matty was furiously digging her in the ribs and flicking her eyes back and forth: Lol had taken a packet of crisps from her bag and was cramming them, two and three at a time, into her mouth. She saw Jo looking and held out the bag.

'Want one?'

'No, thank you,' said Jo. 'I've just had breakfast.'

Matty, pointedly, said: 'Don't you eat breakfast?'

'Yes, but I get hungry,' said Lol. 'If I don't have something before classes my stomach starts rumbling.'

'You obviously don't eat enough,' said Matty. She said it with a perfectly straight face: Lol took it seriously.

'I can't eat a lot at a time, I have a very small appetite. I'm what's known as a picker . . . people *think* I eat a lot,' said Lol, crumpling her empty crisp packet and lobbing it into a bin, 'but really all I'm doing is just picking. Do you want a bite of banana?'

Crisps *and* banana! Jo shook her head. People who kept stuffing themselves (Lol could call it 'just picking' if she liked) deserved to get fat; and if then it made them crabby so that they got themselves thrown out of gangs it was entirely their own fault. Other people didn't have consciences about them, why should she?

Barge and Bozzy weren't yet in the classroom, but Fij was there, frantically finishing off her Maths homework ready for Mrs Stanley.

'Do you want to copy mine?' said Jo.

'Yes!' Fij grabbed at it.

'It's probably not right –'

'Doesn't matter! So long as I've got *something*.'

Fij and Jo had their desks next to each other. Last term, when some people had been new and others had come up from the Homestead, Miss Lloyd had decreed that they should sit in alphabetical order. She had been so pleased with the result – Barge, a talker, next to Claire, a non-talker; Bozzy, a giggler, next to Naomi, dead serious – that to some people's disgruntlement she had announced they could stay like that for the rest of

18

the year. Jo was one of the few who were happy with the arrangement.

'Have you decided –' Fij scribbled, furiously – 'about you-know-what?'

'Yes.' Jo threw a furtive glance over her shoulder, but Lol was busy doing things under her desk lid. (Surely not eating *again*?) 'I'd like to, please.'

'Oh, brilliant! We wanted you, you know, all along.'

It was incredibly flattering. From now on, thought Jo, happily settling into her desk, she need never worry again about being on her own. She and Fij would be a pair, like Barge and Bozzy. They would sit next to each other and do things together and partner each other in hockey and gym.

'What –' She couldn't bring herself to say, *What happens about Lol*? It would have cast a blight on her happiness. 'What happens next?'

'Oh! Well, next we have to have a meeting and make you properly one of us. I'll have a word with Barge. I should think –' Fij lowered her voice, so that Jo had to lean towards her in order to hear. She felt like a conspirator. 'I should think in the lunch hour would be best.'

Jo knew why she said 'in the lunch hour': it was because on Mondays at one o'clock there was Junior choir practice and Big Lol was a member of the choir. She and Matty were the only two from 1N who were.

'But that's not to say,' went on Fij, passing back Jo's Maths book, 'that you can't join us at break. I mean, having a meeting is only a – a wotsit, a –' she wafted a hand – 'a thingummy, a – oh, you know!'

'A formality?' said Jo.

'Yes! A formality. That's all it is.'

It may have been only a formality but at break Big Lol was there, flolloping about, eating her mid-morning bun, still thinking she was a member of the Gang, not knowing what fate had in store for her, and Jo just couldn't bring herself to go and join in. *Nobody* attached themselves to the Laing Gang except by special invitation. Lol would wonder what was going on and why she hadn't been consulted. Jo preferred to trail round with Melanie and Ash, even if it did mean having to listen to fifteen minutes of Melanie telling them how she had gone to watch 'my-uncle-who-is-an-actor' filming on the set of a new soap called *Families*. (The story had been interesting first time round, but this was at least the fifth time Jo had heard it.)

'One o'clock by Dobbsy's shed,' hissed Barge in Jo's ear, as the bell called them back for classes. 'Or the games cupboard,' she added, 'if it's raining.'

It wasn't raining. Jo ate her lunch sitting with Melanie and Ash – 'All those houses that look real, they're just pretend. When you see people indoors, it's all done in the studio. F'r instance, that scene the other day with my uncle and Pen Carlow . . .' She saw Lol, sitting with the Laing Gang, tucking into a hug plateful of spaghetti. She thought, 'It's like the condemned man having his last meal' and suddenly the jacket potato she was eating started to taste like cardboard stuffed with cotton wool and roll about her mouth.

'– my uncle,' said Melanie.

'What?' said Jo.

'My uncle! Did you see him?'

'See him?'

Ashley said, 'Last night. On the television.'

'Oh. No, I don't think I did,' said Jo. She saw Lol suck the last few loops of spaghetti into her mouth and push her chair back. It was time for choir practice: Matty had already gone.

'. . . absolutely *gorgeous*,' said Ashley.

Jo made a vague mumbling sound at the back of her throat. She watched as Barge skewered up her last few chips, and Fij emptied her glass of orange juice. Barge looked across at Jo and solemnly nodded. That was it! The signal she had been waiting for.

'Scuse me,' she said. She scraped back her chair.

'But you haven't finished your lunch!' squeaked Ash.

'And I haven't finished telling you about my uncle,' said Melanie.

'Sorry!' gasped Jo. 'I've got to go!'

As she scurried off in the wake of Barge and the others, she heard Melanie's voice, clear and carrying: 'Poor thing! I just hope she makes it in time . . . an accident would be *too* embarrassing.'

Jo's cheeks flared crimson. It didn't do to upset Melanie. Her wrath might not be as devastating as that of Barge, but her revenge was far more subtle.

Outside in the playground she followed the others – keeping a respectful distance, as befitted a new recruit – across to the playing field, to Mr Dobbs's hut. Mr Dobbs was the caretaker and groundsman. They were not supposed to call him Dobbsy, but everyone did (though not to his face). The hut was locked, so they couldn't go in there – in any case it would be more than their lives were worth: Mr Dobbs was noted for the ferocity of his temper – but at the back was a fallen tree from last year's

21

gales. Provided no one had already bagged it, it made a good sitting-place and was relatively private.

'We just have to keep on eye out for second years,' said Barge.

The second years, it seemed, were under the ludicrous impression that the fallen tree belonged to them.

'Can you imagine?' spluttered Bozzy. 'Owning a *tree* trunk?'

'Simply because they happened to be here when it fell! On that basis,' boasted Barge, 'I could lay claim to half the trees on Petersham Common.'

'Why?' said Fij, interested. 'Where you there when half of *them* fell?'

'Over the years,' said Barge. 'Considering we live on the edge of the place I think I can safely say that in all probability I have seen more trees fall than *most* people in this establishment . . . certainly more than Jan Hammond and her grotty little crew. So if the new recruit would kindly perch herself at this end and keep her eyes peeled –'

'If you sort of bunch yourself up,' said Fij, 'you can see across the playing field and will be able to warn us of approaching danger.'

Jo obligingly bunched herself.

'Good,' said Barge. 'Now we can get down to business. A-hem!' She cleared her throat, with a horrid scraping noise. 'Fellow members, we are gathered here today –'

Jo wriggled, nervously, at the end of the tree trunk. She hadn't realised it was going to be quite that formal.

'We are gathered here today,' intoned Barge, in the

22

dirge-like tones used by Miss Walters, the Head Mistress, at the start of morning assembly, 'for the purpose of purging ourselves of one who is not, and never truly has been, One of Us, and admitting to our ranks one who it is sincerely and genuinely believed by all three of the Rest of Us – to wit, Chloë Julia Boswood, Felicity Isobel Jarvis, and myself, Margery Anne Laing –'

Barge stopped; probably because she had lost the thread of what she was saying.

'To whit to whoo,' crooned Bozzy, mindlessly.

'What we are here for,' whispered Fij in comforting fashion to Jo, who was starting to grow rather alarmed, 'is simply to enrol you in place of Lol.'

Jo nodded, not daring to take her eyes off the playing field lest the dread figure of a Second Year appear. It wasn't very comfortable being all bunched up, but it was a small price to pay for being made a member of the Laing Gang.

'Joanne Jameson, what is your second name?' demanded Barge.

'Um . . . Beverley,' said Jo.

'*Beverley*? What kind of a name is Beverley?'

'Well, it's my grandmother's name, actually.'

'How extraordinary!'

'Why?' said Fij. 'What's extraordinary?'

'A *grandmother* . . . called *Beverley*. I mean they're usually Mary, or Elizabeth, or –'

'Does it really matter?' Fij sounded exasperated. 'Can't we just get on? Break will be over if we're not careful and we shan't have got anywhere.'

'Quite right,' said Barge. 'Let's put it to the vote . . .

23

who votes for Joanne Beverley Jameson to become One of Us?'

Jo risked a quick glance over her shoulder and saw Fij and Bozzy both putting their hands in the air.

'That's it, then,' said Barge. 'You are now officially a member – and will, of course, be expected to behave accordingly. That means –'

'Never mind what it means,' said Fij, hastily. Once Barge got started it was almost impossible to stop her. 'Jammy knows what it means. Let's decide what we're going to do about Lol.'

'Yes,' said Barge. 'Lol. Well –'

There was a silence.

'She'll have to be told,' said Fij.

'Well, obviously.'

'The question is, by who?'

Another silence. Jo had an uncomfortable feeling that eyes were boring into the back of her neck. She decided to say nothing in the hope that they would go away.

'Seems to me,' said Bozzy, 'seems to me that it ought to be Jam . . . seeing as she's the one pushing her out.'

A tremor ran through Jo. It must have communicated itself to Fij, sitting next to her.

'It's not Jammy that's pushing her out,' said Fij. 'It's us that's doing that.'

'Yes, but Jam's the newest.'

'But it was our idea . . . why don't we draw lots, or something?'

'*I* know what we'll do.' Barge's voice: the voice of authority. 'We'll write to her. Who's got a pen and paper?'

Jo fished a small notebook out of her blazer pocket, Fij provided a pen.

'What shall we write?' said Bozzy. She looked at Barge. Barge looked at Fij. Fij, obligingly, said: 'Dear Lol –'

'*Dear Lol*,' wrote Barge, in her big bold handwriting, made slightly uneven from the fact that she was having to rest the very tiny notebook on a small bit of tree trunk.

'It is with deep regret –'

'. . . *deep regret* . . .'

'That we write to inform you –'

'. . . *write to inform you* . . .'

'That as from today –'

'. . . *as from today* . . .'

'You are no longer One of Us.'

'. . . *One of Us*.'

'We are very sorry but you just didn't fit. Signed, etc.'

'Signed *Etcetera*?' said Bozzy.

'Etcetera. It's Latin. It means –'

'I know what etcetera means, thank you very much! You are not the only one who learns Latin. Mensa a table, puella a girl. Amo amas amat. I still don't see,' said Bozzy, 'why we shouldn't sign it with our own names. Won't know who it comes from, will she, if we just put etcetera?'

Jo could feel, rather than see, Fij rolling her eyes. It was Fij who dictated the letter, Barge who wrote it down. Jo wanted no part in it. She had to sign – they all, including Fij, insisted that she sign – 'You're One of Us now.' She knew she was being a coward. She couldn't have it both ways – she couldn't be part of the Gang *and* wash her hands of the horrible business of giving Lol the elbow – but she did wish it were over.

First thing after lunch on a Monday, 1N had CDT with

Mr Roberts. Last term in CDT Jo had made a wooden beetle: this term she was making a cat-faced clock.

'You can work next to me now,' said Fij. Fij was also making a clock; she was experimenting with one in the shape of a blackberry. 'What do you think?' She displayed it, proudly, to Jo. 'Do you think I could patent it?'

'Don't see why not,' said Jo. It was practically impossible to tell where the hands were pointing, but it was an interesting shape.

Out of the corner of her eye she saw Lol come into the studio with Matty, late back from choir practice. Frantically she started babbling. 'You could patent a whole *load* of shapes . . . you could have strawberry clocks and water melon clocks and – and *dandelion* clocks,' said Jo, on a sudden desperate burst of inspiration as Lol loomed up in front of them.

'Hey, you're in my place!' said Lol. 'That's my place, next to Fij.'

Help me! thought Jo. Do something, someone!

Barge came to her rescue. 'You had better read this,' she said, handing Lol the page torn from Jo's notebook.

'Why? What is it?' Lol's face, normally a healthy pink, had grown pastry-coloured. Almost, thought Jo, as if she knew – as if it were something she had been half expecting.

'Just go away,' said Barge, quite kindly, for Barge, 'and have a read of it.'

Lol took the note and moved across to the far side of the studio into a spare place next to Claire, who was making herself a pair of ballet shoes. Jo watched as Lol unfolded the scrap of paper which Barge had handed her. She didn't want to watch, but once she had started she found she was unable to stop. It was the same horrible kind of fascination that made you go on picking at scabs and squeezing at spots, even though you knew it was going to be painful and make you feel sick.

Lol read the note. She did it very slowly and carefully. Jo could see her eyes moving to and fro across the paper. Sweat poured down her face. Her lips pursed as she blew out a great breath. Then she dragged her handkerchief from her sleeve and began mopping, mopping, mopping at her forehead with it.

The memory of Lol mopping her forehead, thought Jo, would be with her as long as she lived.

4

The January term was going to be a good one. Already it had a good feel to it. For their third week of hockey they had been allowed to play a proper game. Afterwards, Miss Dysart had singled out just four of them – Nadge, Jo and Fij from Nellie's, Lee Powell from York – and advised them to try for their House Under-13 teams.

'You should all stand a good chance.'

Nadge, meanwhile, with the help of Jo and Fij, had worked out the form team and pinned a notice on the form notice board:

Goalkeeper	… … …	Laurel Bustamente
Right Back	… … …	Margery Laing
Left Back	… … …	Ashley Wilkerson
Right Half	… … …	Emma Gilmore
Centre Half	… … …	Gerry Stubbs
Left Half	… … …	Chloë Boswood
Right Wing	… … …	Jo Jameson
Right Inner	… … …	Sally Hutchins
Centre Forward	… … …	Nadia Foster
Left Inner	… … …	Matty McShane
Left Wing	… … …	Felicity Jarvis

Claire, of course, refused to play, and the rest – Naomi, Melanie, Julie-Ann and Pru Frank – were all quite useless; but with herself in the centre and Jo and

28

Fij on the wings, and with Barge as right back, said Nadge, they had the makings of a really strong team. Barge on the hockey field was like a tank gone into overdrive. It was a terrifying sight to see Barge bearing down on you, stick raised ready to thwack. Miss Dysart had already had to remind her, 'The aim is to hit the *ball*, Margery, not your opponents!'

As well as being in the form hockey team (which actually it would have been quite difficult *not* to be) and advised to try for the House, Jo had also had an essay returned to her marked 'Highly original! Well done;' Mrs Stanley had said she was 'at long last' starting to show some grasp of elementary mathematics, and just the other day, in special gym class, she had managed her first cartwheel on the beam.

She knew she could never be as brilliant as Nadge, who most probably had started doing back flips in her cradle and could walk on her hands the whole length of the gym, but everybody agreed that Nadge was some kind of athletic genius. Miss Daley had said that if she really cared to work at it Nadge could achieve 'great things' as a gymnast.

Nobody doubted it. But it was funny about Nadge: she didn't seem to want to achieve great things. Unlike Claire, who had ballet lessons six days a week and knew exactly where she was going in life (right to the very top), Nadge wanted only to have a good time. She said that enough black people had distinguished themselves in the field of sport, she didn't see why she should be expected to spend all her free hours in training. Nadge wanted to have *fun*.

Barge, who didn't care to engage in any activity unless

29

there was a prize to be won or points to be gained, said that what Nadge lacked was the competitive urge, and that without the competitive urge you couldn't hope to get anywhere in life; but Jo – thinking of those people who did have competitive urges, such as Barge and Claire, and even, possibly, Gerry Stubbs, who couldn't bear not to come top of every exam she ever took – had the feeling that competitive urges didn't always make people awfully pleasant.

Barge, for instance, could be quite horridly pushy, and Gerry, last term, had gone into a positive sulk when Naomi had beaten her in a Maths test. People without the urge were really far more comfortable. Nadge wouldn't be Nadge if she were all high-powered and ruthless.

Jo wondered about herself. Was *she* competitive? On the whole, she didn't think that she was. What Jo enjoyed was not just the sense of achievement, highly satisfying though that was, but the sense of belonging. Last term she had been a New Girl and still not quite accepted: this term even Nadge (and you couldn't get more popular than Nadge) was automatically including her.

It helped, of course, being part of the Laing Gang. No longer Jo-on-her-own but Jammy, of Bozzy, Jammy, Fij and Barge. People from other Houses knew who she was and pointed her out – 'That's Jo Jameson. She's one of the Laing Gang.' The four of them went everywhere together, did everything together, had secrets which no one else knew about, regularly held meetings in the games cupboard (if it was wet) or behind Mr Dobbs's hut, if dry. Being part of a group, thought Jo, gave one a nice, safe, cosy feeling. A feeling of security. It also, since one no longer had to worry about who one was going to sit with or spend the lunch break with, gave one a great deal more time to devote to really important matters such as practising hockey or thinking of something to write for the school magazine.

Thinking of something for the magazine was growing rather urgent. Entries had to be in by the tenth week of term, and three of those weeks had already gone. Seven weeks might seem like for ever when you calculated the number of Maths lessons they contained, but, as Fij pointed out, '*Some* writers have been known to take as long as seven weeks just deciding where to put a comma.'

'On the other hand,' said Barge, 'some people can write whole books in that time.'

'I suppose it depends whether we are aiming to produce a Work Of Literature or something which people are actually going to read.'

'Oh, I think definitely the latter,' said Barge. 'There is absolutely no point in knocking ourselves out over *works of literature* when half the people in this establishment –' she gave a small, scornful laugh – 'are quite incapable of making any distinction between Jeffrey Archer and Peter Rabbit.'

'Who is Peter Rabbit?' said Bozzy.

'You see?' Barge turned, triumphantly, to Jo. 'You see what I mean? That is precisely the sort of ignorance we are up against!'

'She must mean *Roger* Rabbit,' hissed Bozzy, to Fij.

'I do not mean Roger Rabbit, and I don't mean Bugs Bunny, either. Though I dare say,' added Barge, 'that

31

there would still be some people who might not know the difference.'

'Between Bugs Bunny and Roger Rabbit?'

'No! Between Bugs Bunny and Jeffrey Archer, you idiot!'

'So, what,' said Fij hastily, before one of Barge and Bozzy's slanging matches could break out, 'are we going to aim for? Precisely?'

'Well, preferably something without any commas for a start, since we can't afford to waste seven weeks deciding where to put them. And even if we did it would almost certainly be wrong.'

Miss Lloyd had witheringly informed them, only yesterday morning in English, that their methods of punctuation were slapdash and meaningless: 'You seem to imagine you can just take a handful of commas and sprinkle them around like grass seed.'

'Preferably,' said Barge, 'something without any punctuation at *all*.'

'Like poetry,' said Bozzy.

'Poetry has punctuation!'

'Not all of it.'

'Some of it does. Some of it's absolutely *smothered* in it.'

'So we could write some of the sort that isn't. All we'd have to do,' said Bozzy, 'is just go to the library and find some old book that nobody reads and take a bit out of it and chop it into chunks and call it something like *Fang* or *False Teeth* or *Turbulence* and I bet they'd take it like a shot.'

'You don't think, do you,' said Fij, 'that that could be classed as cheating?'

'Cheating? How can it be cheating? Look at Shakespeare!' cried Bozzy, who never went anywhere near Shakespeare if she could possibly avoid it. 'He stole every single *one* of his plots!'

'Yes, but what you are saying is that we should steal the actual *words*.'

'Well –' Bozzy humped a shoulder. 'If you can come up with any better suggestion –'

Silence, while they racked their brains.

'Is it supposed to be a joint effort?' said Jo.

'It doesn't have to be, but obviously, with four of us working at it we are bound to stand four extra chances of having it accepted.'

It sounded logical, except that Jo felt there was a flaw in it, somewhere. She had seen some of Barge and Bozzy's efforts at English; and as one who had recently had an essay returned marked *Highly Original* . . . 'Imagine,' she said, 'if we were to write four *different* things and they accepted all four of them . . . imagine the House points we'd get!'

'Well, there is that,' agreed Barge.

House points were important. At the end of the summer term they were all added up and the House who had gained the most was given the Dorothy Beech cup (donated in memory of a distinguished Old Girl). The current holders were Sutton's. They had in fact held it for the past three years, but with the arrival upon the scene of the Laing Gang, and more particularly of herself, Barge confidently predicted that 'this year we shall see a change'.

'Jam is quite right,' she said. 'It's House points we should be thinking of. Let us gird up our wotsits,' said

Barge, 'and pull out our fingers and get down to work . . . I vote we have another meeting in a week or so to show each other what we've done. Or at any rate,' she added, seeing Bozzy's mouth start to open, 'to show what we are *planning* to do. It's a pity none of us can draw. They always go for drawings. Doesn't tax the editorial brain the same as having to read words, I suppose.'

'Lol can draw,' said Fij.

'Yes, but Lol isn't one of us.'

'It would still be points for the House,' urged Jo.

'Yes, but she isn't *one* of us.' Barge repeated it, irritably. She had an unshakable conviction that she was surrounded by nincompoops and half-wits; or maybe, in this case, she thought Jo was slyly trying to get Lol edged back in and make themselves five – which is what they never had been and never would be and really one was surprised that a raw recruit, and a New Girl at that, would even dare to suggest it. 'We shall all go away,' decreed Barge, 'and think what we are going to do.'

On the way back across the Field, while Fij was relaying to Barge in immense and mind-blowing detail the plot of last night's episode of *Families* (in which Melanie's uncle had appeared) Bozzy sidled up to Jo and said, 'Would you mind telling me something?'

'What?' said Jo.

'Would you mind telling me what Barge was talking about girders for?'

Jo blinked. 'I didn't know she was.'

'Well, she was,' said Bozzy. 'You can't have been listening . . . we must girder our wotsits.'

Jo struggled for a moment with an unseemly fit of the giggles.

'You've gone all red!' said Bozzy. 'Is it something rude?'

'Um – n-no,' said Jo. 'I d-don't think so. I think what she meant was, we must gird up our loins.'

'Loins?' said Bozzy. 'What's loins?'

Now that she stopped to think about it, Jo really hadn't the faintest idea.

'Sounds rude to me,' said Bozzy.

It did, actually; it sounded very rude.

Jo and Bozzy reached the gate which led from the playing field back into school and stood waiting for the other two to catch up. Jo saw Lol coming up the path towards them: Lol saw Jo at the same moment. She immediately stopped, plunged a hand into her pocket, pulled it out again, puckered her lips and turned back, down the path, making a great display of searching for something. Lol wasn't a very convincing actress. It was obvious to Jo that she simply hadn't wanted to come into contact with her and Bozzy. She supposed that if she had been Lol she wouldn't have wanted to come into contact with her and Bozzy; not after the way they had treated her.

'There goes the Lollipop,' said Bozzy. She giggled. 'It'll be pop goes the Lollipop one of these days, if she doesn't stop stuffing herself!'

Jo smiled, but only because you had to, to be polite. There was nothing worse than making a joke and nobody laughing – unless it was being the butt of a joke and *everybody* laughing.

'Lolli-pop, Lolli-pop,' chanted Bozzy, doing little hops and twirls. 'Pop goes the Lolli-pop . . .'

'Let's get on move on,' said Jo, 'or we'll be late.'

* * *

On Saturday evening Jo's parents went out for a meal to celebrate their wedding anniversary. They left Jo and Tom at home, with Andy as babysitter. Tom thought the idea of a babysitter was ridiculous, but Jo, secretly, was glad. She would have hated to be left in the house by herself, with all the after-dark creakings and groanings that went on ('It's only floorboards,' her mum said, but Jo was not sure), and if she had been left alone with Tom they would be bound to quarrel. Sometimes when they quarrelled they punched each other and threw things. It was probably this that Mrs Jameson was thinking about when she bribed Andy to stay in and keep on eye on them.

'You mean he's being *paid* for it?' roared Tom.

'If you think I'd do it for free,' said Andy, 'you must be out of your basket! You don't imagine that I *want* to stay in on a Saturday night, do you? I can think of far more interesting ways of spending my time.'

Tom, going all self-righteous, which was what he sometimes tended to do when he felt he might be on the point of losing an argument, said: 'It happens to be our parents' *wedding* anniversary.'

'Don't worry,' said Mr Jameson. 'I'm sure we'll bring you back some pizza.'

Pizzas were one of the many things that Jo couldn't stand, but she thought perhaps it might not be the right moment for saying so. Fortunately her mother remembered: 'And a bag of chips,' she said, 'for Jo. Now I want you two younger ones to behave yourselves and not give Andy any trouble . . . I do not want to come back and find Jo with a black eye and Tom with half his hair torn out. All right?'

'It's her that gets violent,' said Tom. 'Not me.'

'Only because you provoke her. I shall expect a full report, so be warned!'

'Naffing spy,' grumbled Tom, stomping off to his bedroom to play computer games.

Andy and Jo were left downstairs with the television.

'Andy,' said Jo, after a bit, 'what's loins?' She wouldn't have asked if Tom had been there, just in case it really was rude. Tom would only have sniggered, in a dirty fashion.

'Something down here,' said Andy, pressing his hands into the small of his back.

'Oh.' (So it *could* be something rude.) 'What happens when you gird them?'

'I presume,' said Andy, vaguely, 'that you put a girdle round them.'

Jo thought about it. 'What would that do?'

'Tighten them up?' said Andy. 'Ready for action?'

Ready for writing poems for the school magazine. Jo pulled a piece of fringe down over her forehead and into her eye. She wondered what she could think of to write about that no one else would choose.

At half-past ten her parents arrived back and Tom came hurtling down the stairs.

'Where's my pizza?'

'Half a pizza,' said Mrs Jameson. 'You're not having a whole one at this time of night.'

'Did you enjoy your meal?' said Jo.

'Yes, it was lovely.'

'Where did you go?'

'We went to Alberto's . . . did you know they have a daughter who's in your class?'

'Oh?' Jo sat, cross-legged, on the floor with her box of French fries. 'Who's that?'

'Laurel Bustamente. Is she a friend of yours?'

'No.' Lol wasn't anyone's friend. She had gone round on her own since being cast out of the Gang. But her situation wasn't any different from what Jo's had been, this time last term. Jo had had to cope with it; so could Fat Lollipop.

'Her mother was telling us,' said Mrs Jameson, 'what a bad time she's been having.'

Jo frowned and said nothing, keeping her head bent over her French fries.

'There's this gang of girls, apparently, who've suddenly turned on her. They've been really nasty.'

'Girls are,' said Tom. He cackled and choked on a piece of pizza. Serve him right. Hateful pig.

'Do you know anything about it?' said Mrs Jameson.

Jo struggled for a moment with a craven desire to say no.

'They haven't been nasty,' she mumbled. 'It's just they didn't want her in their gang any more.'

'Ho!' cried Tom, recovered from his choking fit. 'Gang warfare!'

No one took any notice of him.

'You mean they just threw her out?'

'She never really *belonged*.'

'Well, she's extremely upset about it – she didn't want to go in to school last week.'

'Scratch, scratch, scratch,' said Tom, wriggling his fingers. 'Girls are hateful cats.'

'Shut up!' screeched Jo, hurling a chip at him.

'Jo, stop it! Tom, be quiet. Mrs Bustamente said she's

38

seriously thinking of going in to talk to the Head Mistress. She said it's made Laurel quite ill.'

'It's not my fault,' said Jo.

'I don't suggest it was your fault! But I did say that you might take her along to the Youth Club with you some time.' Jo looked up, horrified. 'Oh, now, come on!' said Mrs Jameson. 'It's not much to ask! You could surely do a little thing like that?'

'I'll think about it,' muttered Jo.

5

There were times when mothers really did come up with some horrific ideas. Take Lol to the Youth Club? Matty would think she had gone bananas. In any case, Lol, recently, had started going round with a girl called Antonia Bird from 1R. If she had Antonia Bird she didn't need Jo. Moreover, she probably wouldn't *want* to go to the Youth Club with Jo – she probably wouldn't want to go anywhere with Jo. Jo was the person who had usurped her.

'That Lollipop,' said Bozzy, at break on Monday afternoon. 'She's breaking all the rules.'

'What rules?' said Jo.

'Going round with someone from another House.'

Nadge went round with someone from another House; but Nadge was Nadge, and was allowed to break rules.

'It's better her going round with someone from another House than not going round with anyone at all,' said Jo.

'Why?'

'Well, because –' Because that way it meant Jo didn't have to feel guilty.

'It's treachery,' said Bozzy. 'You don't go talking to the enemy in times of war.'

'Is it times of war?'

'Well, of course it is! Us against Them . . . they'd use any dirty trick,' said Bozzy, 'to get one up on us.'

Antonia Bird didn't look the sort of girl to use dirty tricks. She was thin and pale and very nearly not there – the sort of girl whom you felt could quite easily disappear one day and nobody would notice.

'Perfect for a spy,' said Bozzy.

Except that it was hard to imagine what she could be spying on. Jo couldn't help feeling, sometimes, that Barge and Bozzy were just the tiniest bit over the top. She had once ventured to suggest as much, but Bozzy had just stared at her, rather piercingly, and said, 'Over *what* top?' while Barge had loftily informed her that 'It is our duty, as loyal members of this House, to be constantly on guard.'

'Let's follow,' hissed Bozzy, 'and see where they go.'

Jo really would have preferred not to, but Fij, her usual ally, had gone to the office with a nosebleed (Barge was being kept in over a little matter of French homework which she variously claimed had been lost, stolen, torn up and sicked over by the dog) and as the newest recruit she hardly liked to set herself up against Bozzy.

'C'mon!'

Bozzy grabbed at Jo's sweater. Together they scuttled crabwise across the playground in the wake of Lol and Antonia Bird.

Lol and Antonia settled themselves on a seat: Jo and Bozzy secreted themselves behind a convenient tree. Jo felt foolish, stuck behind a tree. People would wonder what on earth she was doing there. Bozzy, quite shamelessly, was pressed up against the trunk, peering round with one eye at Lol and the spy, doing her best to hear what they were saying. They heard the spy murmuring something in her low, spy-type voice, then Lol, a bit indistinct, as if she had her mouth full: 'I've been to Austria. I've been all over. This year –' chomp, scrunch, munge – 'we're going to Florida.' Glop. 'On Concorde.'

Bozzy looked round at Jo. Her blue saucer eyes had widened, disbelievingly, to the size of soup plates: 'Concorde!'

Jo shrugged. It was just Lol, showing off. She loved to boast about the places she had been to.

It was really boring, standing behind the tree trunk listening to Lol reel off lists of names. She sounded like a Geography lesson. (Geography was one of Jo's *least* favourite subjects.) It was a relief when the bell rang calling them back to class, though even then they had to wait until Lol and the spy had moved off.

'Look!' Bozzy's hand closed with vice-like grip over Jo's wrist. Jo looked where she was pointing: a twisted scrap of paper lay beneath the seat.

'*That* wasn't there before,' said Bozzy.

The scrap of paper turned out to be a wrapper from a chocolate bar. What had Bozzy expected it to be? A secret communication?

'You never know,' said Bozzy. 'They were obviously talking in some kind of code . . . I mean, *Con*corde! For goodness' sake! Not even Fat Lollipop flies on Concorde.'

'So –' Jo said it carefully. Bozzy could be touchy if she suspected people of not taking her seriously – 'what do you suppose they were *really* talking about?'

'Oh! Could be anything. She was probably trying to

find out what we are going to write for the school mag.'

'But Lol wouldn't know that,' said Jo, 'would she?'

'She would if she'd been eavesdropping on us . . . she could have become a double agent. She could have been a double agent all along.'

'Yes –' Jo struggled for a moment with an untimely giggle which had risen into her throat and was threatening to choke her. She swallowed and forced it back down. 'So have you decided yet what you're going to write?'

'I'm going to write a poem,' said Bozzy. 'In Latin,' she added. 'But don't tell anyone, I want it to be a surprise.'

It would be a surprise, thought Jo. In their most recent Latin test Bozzy had distinguished herself by coming bottom, with two out of twenty-five.

'It's all right,' said Jo. 'You can trust me. I won't tell a soul – not even Barge.'

'Specially not Barge. She'd only go and pinch the idea for herself, and I cannot imagine,' said Bozzy, 'that they are very likely to want *two* poems in Latin.'

It crossed Jo's mind that they were not very likely to want one poem in Latin, but she refrained from saying so. She was all for stamping on big-headedness, but she didn't believe in wantonly crushing people's perfectly harmless pretensions. If Bozzy wanted to try and write a poem in Latin, let her do so. They could but sling it back at her.

'What are you going to do?' said Bozzy.

'Oh –' Jo waved a hand, airily. She hadn't yet got around to thinking about it. 'I shall probably turn out a piece of epic verse, or something.'

On Tuesday evening Jo's mother said: 'Did you talk to Laurel Bustamente about the Youth Club yet?'

'No.' Jo scowled down at her baked beans on toast. (She hated baked beans on toast. They made the toast go all limp and soggy, like a piece of cardboard left out in the rain.) 'You didn't say I *had* to.'

'But it would be nice if you did.'

It wouldn't be nice, it would be horrid. She wouldn't have minded asking Fij, but Fij lived too far away, right over on the other side of town. She had to come in to school by train. Fat Lollipop – unfortunately – had turned out to live only a five-minute car journey away.

'I must say I'm very disappointed in you,' said Mrs Jameson. 'I never thought you'd be so unkind. There's this poor child, without any friends –'

'She has got a friend. She's going round with a girl called Antonia Bird.'

'Oh. Well – all right, then. If you're sure. But I still don't think it was much to ask!'

By Thursday, Lol had stopped going round with Antonia Bird and was on her own again. Jo, changing after a special gym class, found her sitting by herself in a dark corner of the cloakroom. She looked suspiciously as if she had been crying, though she took out her handkerchief and began coughing and blowing her nose as soon as she saw Jo. Jo would have liked to walk away without saying anything, but it wasn't really possible.

'You'll cop it,' she said, 'if Wendy finds you.' Wendy Armstrong was the prefect on cloakroom duty. (People weren't supposed to hang around in the cloakrooms.)

'I don't feel very well,' said Lol. She blew her nose, defensively. 'I think I'm getting a cold.'

'Lots of people have got colds,' said Jo. 'My dad's got a cold.'

'I shouldn't really have come in, only I didn't want to miss classes. I hate to miss classes, specially when it's music. I feel so sorry for Mrs Elliott . . . it must be so *awful* for her, having to teach a load of people that aren't musical.'

They weren't *all* not musical. Claire wasn't, and neither was Matty. But Jo accepted the charge for herself; and for Fij and Bozzy, and for Barge. Perhaps most of all for Barge. Someone had once said of Barge that she had a voice like a pneumatic drill – 'Makes your teeth rattle and your head feel as if it's going to drop off.'

'Your mum and dad came into our restaurant the other night,' said Lol.

'Yes, I know. It was their wedding anniversary.'

'Did they enjoy it?'

'Yes,' said Jo.

'It's a good restaurant,' said Lol. 'You get value for money at our restaurant. My dad does the cooking. He's a fantastic chef. He trained in one of the best hotels in London.'

'My mum said the food was good,' said Jo. Her mum had also said that she should ask Lol along to the Youth Club. *I never thought you'd be so unkind* . . . She looked at Lol's tear-stained face.

'If you're not doing anything on Friday –' Jo's heart sank even as she heard herself say it – 'do you want to come along to our Youth Club?'

'Lollipop?' said Matty. 'To the *Club*? Have you gone demented or something?'

'I felt sorry for her,' said Jo.

'Dunno why you want to feel sorry for that fat thing.'

'Well, I just thought it must be so horrid for her, not having any friends.'

'What you got to ask yourself,' said Matty, 'is *why* she doesn't have any friends.'

Jo already had asked herself, and hadn't been able to come up with any very satisfactory answer. It couldn't just be because she was fat; people weren't *that* mean. And she wasn't anywhere near as bossy as Barge or as aggressive as Bozzy. And *no*body could be as self-righteous as Gerry Stubbs, and Gerry had friends. There was just something about Lol which turned people off.

'You can be friends with her *if* you like,' said Matty, tossing her corkscrew curls. '*I'm* not gonna be.'

'I don't want to be friends with her, exactly. I just felt sorry for her.'

'You mean you just felt guilty,' said Matty. She stood in front of the dressing table in Jo's bedroom, looking at Jo through the mirror. 'It's stupid; she's not worth it. Even Toni Bird got sick of her. D'you know what she told her? That Lol? D'you know what she said? She said Barge and that were jealous, 'cause of all the things she's got and all the places she's been to and her parents having this restaurant and everything and that's the reason they chucked her out.'

Jo frowned. 'How do you know that's what she said?'

''Cause Toni told Susie and Susie told Lee –'

And Lee had told Nadge, and Nadge had told Matty, and now Matty was telling Jo. How people did gossip, thought Jo.

'– and Lee told me and Jool,' said Matty.

Well, at least Nadge hadn't been involved. Nadge was above petty whisperings and backbiting.

'Anyway,' said Matty, 'if –'

She was interrupted by the ringing of the front door bell.

'That'll be her now,' said Jo. She ran to the window and peered out, in time to see a big silver-coloured car pulling away from the kerb. Lol's mum must have brought her. Her dad would be in his restaurant, cooking. 'I s'pose we'd better go down.'

'Honestly,' grumbled Matty, 'you don't half do stupid things at times.'

Jo felt like retorting, 'What's stupider about bringing Lol than bringing Jool?', which was what Matty usually did, though not tonight because Jool had gone to the dentist. She supposed that what was stupider was that Jool and Matty were a couple whereas Jo and Fat Lollipop weren't anything, and as far as Jo was concerned didn't want to be anything.

She wouldn't have thought, after the way she had usurped her, that Lol would have wanted them to be anything, but all evening at the Youth Club, Lol clung to Jo's side as if they were stuck fast with Superglue. There was simply no shifting her. Wherever Jo went, Lol went too.

'I'm going to the toilet,' said Jo, at one point.

'I'll come with you,' said Lol.

Jo couldn't understand it. It wasn't as if Lol were shy; talking was one of the things she was for ever being told off about. Miss Lloyd in particular got mad when people sat and talked while she was talking.

'If it's as interesting as all that, Laurel,' she had said

the other day, 'you had better come out here and tell us all about it. You can take over my job. I'm plainly wasting my time.'

Barge and Gerry Stubbs had been furious because even after that Lol had gone on whispering, until in the end Miss Lloyd had given her an order mark, which meant three points against the House.

'Great blabbermouth!' Barge had said, angrily.

Now, although she was still blabbering, she was doing it all at Jo. Why couldn't she go and do it at someone else? Tom, for example; he deserved to be blabbered at. Or Miles, who was Matty's brother. Miles would probably enjoy it, because Miles really was shy. He tended to stand about in corners, by himself. Jo tried pointing him out to Lol.

'Look,' she said. 'There's Miles, all by himself.'

'Who's Miles?' said Lol.

'Matty's brother.'

Lol studied him. 'He doesn't look much like Matty.'

It was true. Matty was pretty – Jo's mum said she was going to grow up to be a real beauty. She had huge dark eyes and very thick curly hair and *cheek*bones. Jo envied Matty her cheekbones. She sometimes thought that she herself didn't have any cheekbones at all. Jo's face was small and round and totally undistinguished. Miles', on the other hand, was long and soulful and a bit lopsided. Miles was what Jo's gran called 'homely'. He had ever so slightly sticking-out teeth and wore heavy horn-rimmed spectacles. Still, Lol was hardly in a position to go round picking holes in people. Miles might be homely but at least he wasn't fat; if anything, he was on the skinny side. Lol, in her baggy tracksuit, looked like nothing so much as an enormous cream puff. It was a pity, really: her face, on its own, wasn't too bad. If it hadn't been for the double chin she would have been quite prettyish in a pink-and-whitey sort of way.

'Miles is really nice,' said Jo. He was Tom's age, but he wasn't foul and sexist like Tom. 'You could go and talk to him.'

If Lol would only go and talk to Miles, it would mean that Jo could go over and attach herself to Tom's crowd. Jo wouldn't normally go anywhere near Tom if it could possibly be avoided, but there was a boy in Tom's class called Robert Wyngarde, commonly referred to by Tom as Robbie. Jo had heard a lot about Robbie. Tom didn't exactly look up to him, because Tom wasn't the sort of boy ever to look up to anyone, but he had made it plain that he thought Robbie was OK.

Last week, for the first time, Tom had brought Robbie to the Club with him. Casually, in passing (but only because it couldn't be avoided) he had introduced him to Jo – 'This is my sister, Jo. Jo, this is Robbie Wyngarde.' Robbie had smiled and said hallo, and Jo had smiled and said hallo back, and that had been that. They hadn't spoken again for the rest of the evening. But this evening Jo had noticed that he kept sending her little looks across the hall. Jo, in return, kept sending little looks of her own (though not when Robbie was sending his: that would have been embarrassing). She had never had a boyfriend and wasn't absolutely certain that she wanted one, but if she ever did have she thought that she would like him to be like Robbie.

He wasn't flash, like Matty's cousin Dee who all the girls went crazy over, but he could definitely be described as good-looking. He was taller than Tom, and not so chunky, and he had springy chestnut-coloured hair; a lock of which kept falling over his forehead and into his eyes (bright blue and twinkly) so that he had to keep batting at it with the back of his hand. Jo loved the way he did that.

'Don't look now,' said Lol, out of the side of her mouth, 'but there's a boy over there who keeps looking at me.'

'Oh? Where?'

'Over there.' Lol nodded sideways with her head, while keeping her eyes firmly on Jo.

Jo turned, pretending to be squinting at the clock at the far end of the hall. She turned back.

'Do you mean Tom? Or do you mean the boy standing next to Tom? The boy standing next to Tom was Tom's best mate, Keith Baxter. Lol could have Keith Baxter and welcome.

'Not him,' said Lol. 'The handsome one with the blue eyes.'

HANDSOME ONE WITH BLUE EYES? That was Robbie!!!

Robbie wasn't looking at Lol, he was looking at Jo. Wasn't he?

'I've got blue eyes,' said Lol. She pushed her face into Jo's. 'See?' Jo recoiled. That's because my mum is Irish. Lots of Irish people have blue eyes. They're very good-looking, Irish people. And Italians. My dad's Italian. My dad –'

Jo felt like screaming. She didn't want to hear about Lol's dad. She had already heard about Lol's dad. She wished Lol would go away and – and *drown* herself. Go and fall into a big fattening vat of chocolate milkshake and *drown* herself.

'. . . fantastic chef,' said Lol. 'My mum –'

Jo resigned herself, glumly, to being stuck with Lol for the rest of the evening. Across the room, Matty, playing table tennis with Nadge, sent her an impish beam. No chance of Matty coming to her rescue. Nobody was going to come to her rescue. This was *horrible*.

6

On Sunday morning Matty came round, with Jool (Matty was lucky: Jool only lived a short bus-ride a way).

'We've come to do my hair,' said Jool. 'Matt's going to plait it for me.'

They wanted to use Jo's dressing table mirror, which had a middle piece and two wings so that you could see yourself sideways and even look at the back of your head.

'All right,' said Jo.

They all trooped upstairs, bumping into Tom on the landing. Tom, being Tom, didn't stand back to let them go past, but simply blundered on, regardless.

'Don't mind us,' said Jo, 'will you?'

'Didn't see you!' yelled Tom, leaping three at a time down the stairs.

Jool giggled. 'Your brother!' she said.

'My brother is a pain,' said Jo.

'All brothers are a pain.' That was Matty confidently leading the way into Jo's bedroom.

'Yours isn't,' said Jo. Matty's brother was gentle and sensitive and quiet: all the things that Tom wasn't. 'Miles isn't a pain!'

'He can be,' said Matty. 'Like on Friday at the Club –' – she pulled the stool out from under Jo's dressing table – 'Hanging around, not talking to anyone. Makes you want to go and shake him. I mean, why can't he just walk up and say hallo like anyone else?'

'He's shy,' said Jo.

'Well, it's stupid,' said Matty. 'At his age.'

Matty didn't understand about people being shy. Since making friends with Jool and being accepted by Nadge and Lee Powell and their lot she had really blossomed.

Jool seated herself at the dressing table. 'I want it in plaits *all over*.'

'It'll be in plaits all over!'

'But I don't want them stuck out. I want them flat.'

'They'll be flat.' Matty took a comb from her pocket and wielded it in business-like fashion. 'Just sit there,' she said, 'and keep still.'

Jool obediently sat still. Jo perched herself on the window seat, from where she could not only watch the progress of the plaiting but also keep an eye on the road. Not that she was expecting anyone to call, but sometimes interesting things happened out there, like the man at number four running his car into his own gatepost and getting out and swearing; and Mrs Dainty, their next door neighbour (on the other side from Matty) running out to hang mothballs round the trunk of her cherry tree so that 'dogs won't use it as a toilet'; and the Rottweiler that lived further up the road promptly coming past and using it as one. Things like that were really funny.

'Matt said you took Lollipop to the Youth Club on Friday,' said Jool.

'Yes.' Jo turned, to look out of the window. She didn't want to talk about Lol and the Youth Club.

'Must be mad,' said Jool.

'I told her she was,' said Matty, 'but she wouldn't listen.'

'You know what'll happen? Don't you? Know what'll happen?'

'What?' Jo spoke without removing her gaze from the (totally empty) road.

'You'll get lumbered with her,' said Jool. 'She's like a leech . . . minute anyone shows any interest and – *slumph*!' Jool made a loud slurping noise. 'That's it, she's hooked herself into you, sucking at your blood . . . I remember one time in the Homestead, Gerry Stubbs asked her to her birthday party and she got stuck with her for a whole *term*.'

'So?' said Jo.

'So Gerry d– *ow*!' yelled Jool. 'You're hurting! Gerry didn't *want* to be stuck with her did she? *No*body wants to be stuck with her . . . I mean, she'd already got Pru, she didn't want anyone else. But you try dropping hints and old Fat Lollipop, she just doesn't take any notice. Gerry had to end up being really rude.'

'Why? What did she say?' asked Matty.

'Told her to push off,' said Jool.

'*Gerry* did?'

'She's like that, Gerry is.'

Jo wondered if she could ever be like that. It was one thing to *feel* like telling Lol to go and drown herself, but she couldn't imagine ever actually doing it.

'There!' said Matty. 'Look!'

Jo looked. Jool's hair, which before had been scraped on top of her head in a silly little sticking-up bunch, was now neatly plaited into dozens of tiny plaits, all the same size.

'That's brilliant!' said Jo.

'Yeah?' Matty sounded modestly pleased. 'P'raps I should take up hairdressing.'

At that moment there was a click as someone opened the front gate. Jo spun round on her window ledge.

'It's Lol!'

'Lol?'

'Coming here –'

'Coming *here*?'

'Up the path –'

'Up the *path*?'

'I told you, I –'

'Quick!'

'– said –'

'*Quick*!'

'What?'

'Hide!'

'Where?'

'Anywhere!'

'Wardrobe!'

Matty, giggling, flung open the wardrobe door and dived inside, followed by an equally giggling Jool.

'Shut us in!'

'You're mad,' said Jo.

'*Shut us in*!'

'Oh, all right.' Jo slammed the wardrobe door. 'Just don't blame me if you suffocate to death.'

Two sets of stifled giggles were her only answer. From downstairs came her mother's voice: 'Jo! Laurel's here. I'm sending her up.'

Stump, stump, stump came Laurel up the stairs. She was wearing a pair of baggy jeans and a checked shirt. By the time she reached the top of the stairs she was puffing.

'I thought I'd just come,' she said, 'and say hallo.'

Jo felt like saying, 'So now you've said it perhaps you'd like to go away again?', but of course she didn't.

'I've brought you this,' said Lol, pushing a flat square box at Jo.

'What is it?' Jo prised open a corner. 'Oh! A pizza. Thank you very much.' She hated pizzas, but Tom and Andy would enjoy it.

'It's one of my dad's. It's got olives on it. I love olives, don't you? I could eat olives all day.'

'I don't think I've ever tasted them,' said Jo.

'Try one!' Lol wrenched the box away from Jo and ripped the lid off. 'Here!' She pushed a shiny black object into Jo's face. Jo really had no alternative but to open her mouth. Ugh! The olive was revolting. All salty and slimy and *yuck*.

'I don't think I like olives,' she said.

Lol said that was probably because she wasn't used to them. Olives, she said, picking another one off the top of the pizza, were an acquired taste. You had to have quite a sophisticated palate to appreciate olives.

'I think actually I have quite a *basic* sort of palate,' said Jo. (Did she really hear another stifled giggle coming from the wardrobe?)

'Let's talk,' said Lol, seating herself on Jo's bed with the pizza.

'What shall we talk about?'

'Anything.'

It wasn't easy, talking to the Lollipop, knowing all the time that Matty and Jool were squashed up in the wardrobe listening to everything that was being said.

Every now and again little snorts and squeaks and snuffles could quite plainly be heard, but fortunately the Lollipop was so busy talking that she seemed not to notice.

'We're doing a musical next term . . . all the people in Mrs Elliott's special music groups. We're doing something called *Ballet Shoes*. Have you heard of it? It's from a book by someone. Someone called Noel something. Stretton, or something.'

'Streatfield,' said Jo. She had borrowed it last term from Claire.

'That's right,' said Lol. 'Something like that. They're holding auditions next week so's we can start on rehearsals straight away after half term . . . I'm going to audition for the part of Posy.'

Posy? 'But Posy was a dancer!' said Jo.

'They're all dancers . . . Pauline, Petrovna, and Posy.' Lol counted them off on her fingers. 'Posy's the youngest, that's why I'm doing her.'

'But won't you have to dance?' said Jo. 'I mean, won't there be scenes where you have to wear a leotard or a tutu or something?'

'What's a tutu?' Lol gouged out another olive from the top of the pizza.

'A sort of frilly ballet dress,' said Jo. From inside the wardrobe came a high squeaking sound. The thought of Lol in a frilly ballet dress was obviously proving too much.

Lol paused, in mid-munch. 'What's that?'

'Must be mice,' said Jo. She walked across and kicked, hard, at the wardrobe door. The squeaking stopped. 'You'd have thought', she said, 'if it's dancers, they'd want people like Claire.'

'It's a *musical*,' said Lol. 'They want people who can sing.'

They might want people who could sing, but how could someone Lol's size play a dancer? Unless, perhaps, it was supposed to be funny, like last term's fairies? It was the only explanation Jo could think of.

Lol stayed for almost half an hour, by which time a large chunk of pizza had been demolished. She would have stayed for longer – all day? – if Jo hadn't suddenly thought of an excuse.

'I'm afraid you'll have to go now, we're going to my auntie's this afternoon.'

It was the most terrible fib. Jo's auntie lived in a place called Bicester, which was *miles* away. They had to leave at nine o'clock in the morning when they went to visit her.

As she took Lol downstairs, Jo had a sudden dreadful thought: suppose Lol said something to mum?

The she had another dreadful thought: suppose Mum said something to Lol? Something about Matty and Jool still being there, and then Lol would ask where, and Mrs Jameson would say, 'They didn't go, did they?' and Jo would have to lie a second time and say yes, and Mrs Jameson would wonder how it could have happened without her knowing, and talk about a tangled web, thought Jo. Once you started making things up there was simply no end to it.

Happily, the only person they met on the way downstairs was Tom, talking on the telephone to someone. (She knew it couldn't be his mate Keith Baxter; he was being far too polite.)

'So I'll see you again next Friday,' said Lol, 'for the Club. Shall I?'

Jo's heart went *thunk* down to her stomach.

'Well,' she said, trying to think of yet another excuse.

'If you like,' said Lol, 'we could stop and pick you up in the car and take you all the way there.'

'Well, but there's Matty, you see. I always go with Matty. And then there might be Jool, as well. And Miles. And Tom.'

'That's all right,' said Lol. 'We can use Dad's car. Dad's car is bigger than Mum's. You can get six people easy in Dad's.'

'Did she say six people?' said Tom, putting down the telephone. 'What is it? A Roller?'

'Don't ask me,' said Jo, shutting the front door.

'Could be a BMW, I suppose . . . or a Merc. Could be a Merc. Or one of them big estates. Why didn't you ask her? You know I'm interested.'

'You can see for yourself,' said Jo, 'next Friday.'

There was a stampede down the stairs: Jool and Matty, giggling. 'She's coming to pick us up,' said Jo.

'Who is?'

'Lol is.'

'*Lol* is?'

'I told you,' began Jool, but thankfully Mrs Jameson appeared from the kitchen before she could get started on her litany. (*I told you she'd stick, I told you you wouldn't be able to get rid of her, I told you she was like a leech . . .*)

'Who wants a cup of hot chocolate?' said Mrs Jameson. 'Matty? Julie-Ann? Come through to the

59

kitchen, all of you . . . where's Laurel? She hasn't gone, has she?'

'She only came just for a few minutes.'

'So how's she going to get home?'

'Dunno. Walk, I s'pose.'

'Do her good,' said Matty. 'Get a bit of the pudding off her.'

'She's like a big sack of blubber,' said Tom, elbowing his way into the kitchen ahead of everyone else.

'Tom Jameson!' His mother caught him by the neck of his sweater, hauling him backwards into the hall. 'Where are your manners?'

What manners? thought Jo. He didn't have any.

'Ladies first,' said Matty, pulling an impudent face at Tom as she walked past him.

'*Guests* first,' said Mrs Jameson. 'And you can just stop being rude about Laurel!'

'Rude?' said Tom. 'Who's being rude? I wasn't being rude! All I said was she looked like a sack of blubber. She does look like a sack of blubber. What's rude about that?'

'You ought to see her in gym,' said Matty.

'No *thank* you!'

'Makes you feel sick, sometimes.'

'It's like she's got *car* tyres,' said Jool. 'All stuck under her skin.'

'Semolina pudding, more like.'

'Yeah, semolina pudding! And it wobbles.'

'Puke!' Tom turned to the sink and began making disgusting noises. Tom was very good at making disgusting noises. It really did sound as though he were being sick. 'Ought to prick her with a pin and watch it ooze out.'

'*Ugh*!' screeched Jool and Matty, enjoying themselves.

'Now, listen!' Mrs Jameson banged a handful of mugs on to the table. 'You just listen to me, all of you . . . you ought to be ashamed of yourselves! Making fun of someone, just because of the way they look. Have you ever stopped to think how it must be to be Laurel? How do you imagine *she* feels every time she has to change for gym? It's all very well for you! Especially you three girls. You're nice and slim –'

Matty looked rebellious. Jool preened. The fact was that Jool *wasn't* slim, she was decidedly pudgy. It was only when compared to the Lollipop that she could be described as slim.

'Imagine how you'd feel if you were Laurel, having to go and buy clothes . . . having to try them on in front of everyone. Imagine being in one of those hideous communal changing rooms and having you three watching her, sniggering – in what I have to say is an extremely *childish* fashion, as well as being very unkind. It's all right for you, you never have to think about things like that.'

'Yeah, but we don't keep stuffing ourselves,' said Matty.

Jo stared at Matty in wonderment. This time last year she would never have dared talk back like that to Jo's mum. She had always been such a meek, mild sort of person. Finding her feet had certainly changed her; Jo couldn't decide whether it was for the better or not.

'Oh, now, come on!' Jo's mum was saying. 'I've seen you and Jo shoving chocolate bars down yourselves!'

'Yeah, but not straight after breakfast,' said Matty. 'I

mean, what I'm saying . . . all right, I know it must be rough on her, like in gym and clothes shops and that, but the thing is, it's her own fault.'

Jool nodded, vigorously. 'It is! She brings it on herself.'

'Fat people always do,' said Tom.

'Oh, shut up, Thomas!' Mrs Jameson took a swipe at him.

'I don't think *all* fat people do.' Matty said it carefully, obviously not wanting to upset Mrs Jameson. 'Maybe there's some fat people can't help it, like if there's something wrong with them or something. But all it is with Lol, she just *eats*.'

Mrs Jameson sighed. 'Yes, well, people eat for all sorts of reasons. It doesn't necessarily make them happy. And you have to remember that her parents run a restaurant. It can't be easy for her. All I'm asking is, just do try to be a bit more understanding. Will you?'

'Yeah.' Matty said it shamefacedly. 'I s'pose so.'

'And you, Jo!'

What did she mean, *and you, Jo*? What about *and you, Jool*? And anyway, it wasn't Jo that had been being horrid, it was Tom and the others. Jo had been quite nice to Lol, up in her bedroom – well, apart from telling her a bit of an untruth and letting Jool and Matty hide in the wardrobe.

'Jo?' Mrs Jameson was waiting.

'I'm already taking her to the Youth Club,' grumbled Jo. 'What else am I expected to do?'

Later that morning, when Jool and Matty had gone home, Tom came up to Jo.

'That was Robbie on the telephone earlier,' he said.

62

'Robbie Wyngarde.'

'Oh, yes?' said Jo, trying not to show too much interest. (It didn't do to show too much interest; Tom was liable to take advantage of it at a later date.) 'What did he want.'

'Wanted to know if you'd be at the Club again on Friday . . . he wanted to talk to you,' said Tom, 'but you'd got Fatso with you and he didn't like to.'

'You're not to call her that!' Jo's cheeks were burning furiously. (So it *had* been her that Robbie was looking at!) 'You heard what mum said . . . we've got to stop being fattist.'

'What's fattist?' said Tom. 'She's fat so I call her Fatso . . . you've got a face like a full moon so I call you Moon Face. I suppose you'd say that's faceist?'

Tom was such a *pain*.

7

Life at school was growing better and better. On Wednesday, because Fij was away having another of her nosebleeds (Fij was always having nosebleeds: she had had one once all over the pages of her *Junior Maths II*), Nadge singled out Jo to help with the composition of the seven-a-side hockey they were planning to play against Sutton's. She could have consulted Barge, she could have consulted Bozzy – after all, they had both been in the Homestead with her; instead she had consulted Jo.

Between them they decided that the team should be:

Nadge (captain)
Fij (vice-captain)
Jo
Barge
Bozzy
Sally Hutchins

plus one more. It was a question of who was to be in goal.

'It might be better,' said Nadge, 'if we put Barge in goal and brought Matty into the side. What do you reckon?'

Jo was torn. Naturally, as Matty was her friend, she would have loved her to be on the team; but that would mean ousting Lol – for the *second* time. Lo seemed to spend her life being ousted.

Jo wished there were a way of keeping Lol as goalkeeper and still having Matty, but there really wasn't anyone else who could be got rid of. The Mouse (Sally Hutchins) might be tiny, but she was fast and deadly. The Mouse couldn't be got rid of. And not even for Matty could she bring herself to suggest dumping either Bozzy or Barge. Barge, in any case, had shock value: one glimpse of her bulk bearing down on them and people tended to go into spasms. And Bozzy, through sheer aggression, was effective out of all proportion to her size.

'I think that's what we'll do,' said Nadge. 'I think we'll leave out the Lollipop and have Barge in goal and that way we can bring Matty in.'

Jo watched, with mixed feelings, as Nadge took out her pen and wrote *Matty McShane* at the end of the list.

'I hope Lol doesn't mind,' she said.

Lol was the one blot on Jo's horizon. She hadn't dared tell any of the others about her coming to the Youth Club. Fij might be hurt, even though she lived too far away to be able to get there. Barge and Bozzy would look at her as if she had taken leave of her senses. They might even accuse her of treason – *doing* things with an outsider. They didn't mind her doing things with Matty, because after all Jo and Matty lived next door to each other and had been best friends before coming to Peter's; besides, Matty wasn't an ex-Gang member.

'I hope she doesn't feel she's being pushed out,' worried Jo.

'Lol's always being pushed out.' Even the easygoing Nadge found it difficult to think of good things to say about Lol. 'It's 'cause she will keep pushing *in*.'

'She didn't push into the hockey team.'

'No, but I don't think she specially cares. She was grumbling the other day about always having to be in goal.'

Jo had heard the Lollipop grumbling. Miss Dysart, who wasn't terribly sympathetic, had said, 'Well, Laurel, you know the solution . . . get some of that weight off and maybe we'll think about putting you elsewhere. But there isn't much point if you can't keep up, is there?'

Jo had felt embarrassed for her. It was such a horridly shaming sort of thing to have said about you, especially in front of everyone. On the other hand it was perfectly true, Lol *couldn't* keep up. Whenever they had to do their two laps round the hockey field before starting on a game, Lol never managed to get more than half-way.

'Hey, you know on Friday?' Nadge, having pinned her hockey team to the notice-board, turned, face alight with mischief, to Jo. 'You know your brother?'

How could she *not*? 'Tom,' she said. What had he done now? Last term, for a short while, he had gone out with Nadge, until he had dropped her in favour of Claire. And much good *that* had done him. He had discovered, as Jo before him, that Claire had no room in her life for anyone or anything outside the ballet.

'You know that boy he brought with him?'

'Robbie?' (Blush, blush.)

'One with blue eyes.'

'What about him?' Jo tried not to sound anxious. Was Nadge going to tell her something she wouldn't want to hear? Like, *he's asked me to go out with him*, or –

'He really fancies you,' said Nadge.

Jo's face promptly transformed itself into a boiled beetroot.

'How d'you know?'

Nadge gave one of her mad cackles. 'I know!'

'Yes, but how? He didn't tell you?'

'Me read signs,' said Nadge. She rolled her eyes, clasped the region of her heart, did a pretend swoon. 'Him Blue Eye . . . Blue Eye fancy Moon Face . . .'

She'd got that from Tom.

'You're crazy,' said Jo.

Nadge *was* crazy, everyone knew that; but even Tom had said that Robbie wanted to talk to her . . .

On Friday evening the Lollipop called round just as she had threatened. She came with her father in his special big car that could seat six people. (It looked like a perfectly ordinary sort of car to Jo, but Tom seemed impressed. 'Cor!' he said. 'This is a bit serious!')

Matty at first wasn't going to come because of waiting for Jool; only then Jool turned up and she didn't have any excuse, though Jo knew why she hadn't wanted to. It was because it made you feel bad, accepting favours from someone you'd been mean about. But it wasn't really possible to say no to Lol's dad. Mr Bustamente was big and jolly and rather handsome in spite of his bigness. All the time he was driving he kept singing songs in Italian. The Lollipop said, 'Dad! You're just showing off.'

'So I'm showing off!' said Mr Bustamente. He took both hands off the wheel and threw them above his head. '*O sole mio* –'

'*Dad*!' screamed Lol. To the others she said, 'He doesn't usually carry on like this. He's just doing it to prove he's Italian.'

'Italiano!' cried Tom.

'Italiano!' cried Lol's dad.

Jo giggled, and so did Jool. Matty smiled, politely. Miles, ever serious, took off his glasses, huffed on them, wiped them with his handkerchief and put them back on.

'My dad's an idiot,' said Lol.

Jo thought that Lol's dad let her get away with far more than her own dad did. She would never dare call her dad an idiot, not even in fun. Tom, thinking he was being clever, had once addressed him as Baldie and received a sharp clip round the ear. No one could have addressed Lol's dad as Baldie: he had a full head of black hair, very thick and curly. (The thought crossed Jo's mind that he was wasted on the Lollipop.)

'Don't forget,' hissed Tom, as they got out of the car, 'Robbie wants to talk to you.'

Talking to Robbie meant getting rid of the Lollipop. Perhaps this week she wouldn't cling quite so much. Perhaps Miles –

She looked round. Lol was still getting out of the car, Miles was hovering by the entrance to the Club, not sure whether to follow Tom (always the first to burst in anywhere) or wait for the others.

'Miles,' said Jo, 'Lol's dying to meet you.' Miles looked at her, uncertainly. 'She is,' said Jo. 'Honestly.'

'But I already met her,' said Miles.

'Not properly! Let me introduce you.' Jo grabbed at the Lollipop as she got out of the car. Miles took a nervous step backwards. 'Lol, this is Miles,' said Jo. 'Miles, this is –'

'He knows who I am,' said Lol. 'We just gave him a lift, didn't we?'

She obviously thought Jo was mad and had forgotten.

'Yes, but I'm *introducing* you,' said Jo. 'People have to be *introduced* – and oh, good heavens!' she said. 'I've just remembered –'

'What?' screamed Lol, as Jo bolted for the entrance.

'Something I've got to do!' yelled Jo.

People could burn in hell for telling lies; but she comforted herself with the reflection that really and truly she was doing Miles a good turn: he needed a girlfriend. (He was another who'd had a thing about Claire, but Claire wouldn't look twice at him. Claire wouldn't look twice at anyone.) By the end of the evening, with any luck, Lol and Miles would have got it together, and it would be Jo they had to thank for it. In any case it wasn't a total lie: there *was* something she had to do.

Tom was in the middle of the room, as usual, chatting with his mates. Keith Baxter was there, with his horrible rabbity teeth and his hair all sticking up like a lavatory brush, and another boy who she didn't know, and a boy called Wally who she did know and couldn't stand, and beautiful, blissful, blue-eyed Robbie who wanted to talk to her.

Tom glanced up and saw Jo standing there. Instead of shouting, 'What d'you want, Moon Face?' in his usual loudmouthed fashion, he raised a hand and imperiously beckoned her over. She wouldn't normally have obeyed such a summons; not from Tom. The only reason she went was because of beautiful Robbie.

Robbie, for all he was so beautiful, turned out to be quite bashful. Not as bashful as Miles, but too bashful to come and talk to her off his own bat –

'I was going to come and say hallo but I could see that you were with your friend.'

'She's not my friend,' said Jo. 'Not really. We just happen to go to the same school.'

School was a safe subject. They managed to talk about school for almost ten minutes. (Out of the corner of her eye, at one point, Jo thought she saw the shadow of big Lol looming, but she couldn't be sure. Purposely she didn't look.) At the end of ten minutes, when they might have started to run out of things to say, Tom rushed over and told them they had to come and play handball – 'You can be on the same side, if you like.'

There were eight people playing handball – Jo and Robbie, Tom and his mates, Nadge, Lee Powell and Susie Fern. They had to go into another room to do it, because that was where the court was marked out. The court was actually a netball court with a tennis court chalked on top of it and a net in the middle. The rules of the game were quite simple: the ball (a tennis ball) was allowed to hit the ground just once and no more. There was nowhere that was offside and a point was scored when the ball entered one of the goal circles on the netball court. It could either roll there or it could be hit there.

'And if you hit it into your own circle it's a point to the other side!'

They played handball for the rest of the evening, until Mrs Barlow, who ran the Club, sent someone to tell them it was time to stop.

'That was fun,' said Robbie. He looked at Jo. 'Will you be here again next Friday?'

'I expect so,' said Jo.

'Then so will I be,' said Robbie.

Jo wondered whether that meant he was her boyfriend. When Tom, for a short time, had been Nadge's boyfriend they had walked through the centre of town together, holding hands. (Jo had seen them, though Tom didn't know it.) She couldn't quite imagine doing that with Robbie, but everyone had to start somewhere and they *had* kept bumping into each other playing handball.

It wasn't until they went back to the main room to join the others that Jo remembered about Lol. Where was she? Her dad had said he would be coming back at the end of the evening to pick her up and give them all a lift.

'If you're looking for Fat Lollipop,' said Matty, 'she already left.'

'She had this quarrel,' said Jool, 'and went flouncing out.'

Jo's eyes wandered involuntarily to Miles. Nobody, surely, could quarrel with Miles? Not even the Lollipop.

'Wasn't Miles,' said Matty. 'It was some bunch of girls from Woodside. I dunno what happened exactly. I think they told her to shove off.'

'She was all crying,' said Jool.

Jo swallowed. 'So how'd she get home?'

'She went and rang her dad.'

'We tried to stop her,' said Matty. 'Even offered to buy her a Coke.'

'Yeah, we did. We tried.'

'You know, like your mum said,' said Matty. 'We weren't mean to her.'

'It was that lot from Woodside. Right rough lot they are.'

Why couldn't she just have stayed with Miles, thought Jo, crossly. Now there would be trouble, because Mrs Jameson would want to know why they hadn't come back in the car and Jo would have to tell her why they hadn't and then she would say that Jo should have looked after her and even though the picture of Lol all crying was slightly disturbing, Jo really couldn't see that it was her fault. She couldn't see why *she* should be expected to play nursemaid. Why not Matty or Jool, or even Tom if it came to that? It wasn't fair, picking on Jo.

As it happened there wasn't any trouble because Mrs Jameson was in the bath and didn't notice the lack of car; it was Jo's dad who opened the door. All the same, Jo did feel a little bit bad about abandoning Lol to Miles (who was obviously a dead loss when it came to girls) and then just forgetting her. She didn't feel *very* bad; but bad enough to get the Bustamentes' telephone number from the telephone book and ring up to ask if Lol were all right.

It was Mrs Bustamente who answered. She said that Lol had come home 'extremely upset . . . some of the girls were very nasty to her.'

'They weren't any people from our school,' said Jo.

Mrs Bustamente said that whoever they were they ought to know better. She said, 'Laurel's in bed at the moment, I'm just going to take her up a sandwich and a glass of milk. I'll tell her you rang. She'll be ever so pleased. I expect she'll be round to see you on Sunday and give you all the details. She needs someone sympathetic to talk to.'

Jo opened her mouth automatically to say 'Oh, but I don't think I shall be here on Sunday, we're going to visit my gran', but Mrs Bustamente had already put down the receiver. In any case, you couldn't *keep* telling lies.

Sunday morning, as usual, Matty came round. She didn't have Jool with her because Jool really *had* gone to visit her gran. Matty wanted to know whether Jo felt like 'going up the woods and doing some photographs?'

Matty was into photography in a big way. Jo had asked for a camera for Christmas and had done her best to get interested, but it was difficult to feel much enthusiasm when every picture you took came out all blodged or blurred or only half there. Matty said that what she needed was practice. (Tom said she must be cross-eyed.)

'So d'you want to?' said Matty.

'Mm.' Jo wrinkled her nose. 'I really ought to stay in and do that Geography homework. *And* there's that essay for M–' She stopped, as the gate clicked. A quick glance out of the window confirmed her fears: 'It's Lol,' she said.

'*Again*?' Matty giggled. 'Shall I get in the wardrobe?'

'No, you keep making noises.'

'I won't make noises. I promise!'

'You will, and anyway it's eavesdropping.'

'Oh!' Matty pulled a face. 'You're getting to be such a *spoil*sport! I'm going.'

As Matty marched out, Lol clumped in. She hadn't brought a pizza with her this time, but two big squidgy buns covered in white icing. Jo nibbled at the icing but left the bun (it was full of currants and Jo couldn't stand currants) while Lol sat on Jo's bed and ate and talked at the same time.

She said that what had happened on Friday was that these girls from Woodside had ganged up on her. They had attacked her and called her names. They had done it because they were jealous, and the reason they were jealous was because her father owned one of the best restaurants in Petersham and the mother of one of the Woodside girls had once worked for him as a waitress and had been given the sack because she wasn't any good, and also because she had been mean to Lol. She had tried bossing her – '*In my own dad's restaurant!*' – and what was more she had taken money out of the till, only no one had ever been able to prove it, but everyone knew it was her, there wasn't anyone else it could have been, and all Lol had done was go up to this girl and remind her of it, because 'It's not right she should get away with it; my mum and dad have had to work really hard to get their own place,' and this girl had 'threatened to punch my face in if I didn't be quiet.'

Reluctantly, by the time Lol had finished, Jo was beginning to understand how the girl had felt.

'So what happened with you and Toni Bird?' she said, trying to change the subject.

'Antonia is very immature,' said Lol. 'Just because I was trying to tell her something about Austria and what it's like to go skiing, she got all jealous and said I was boasting. I *wasn't* boasting. I was just trying to describe it to her because she's never been there.'

'Perhaps she didn't want it described,' said Jo.

'It wasn't that. It was because she was jealous. It's silly of people,' said Lol, 'to get jealous. I can't help it if I'm an only child.'

Jo was still trying to work out what being an only child had to do with it when Lol started off on yet another grievance: why had she been left out of the seven-a-side-hockey? *She* was supposed to be goalkeeper, not Barge.

74

'Nadge thought you didn't like being goalkeeper,' said Jo.

'She might have *asked* me,' said Lol. She reached out from the bed to Jo's half-eaten bun. 'Shall I finish this for you if you don't want it?'

'You oughtn't,' said Jo. 'It's fattening. You'll never lose weight if you keep eating buns and things.'

'Who says I want to lose weight?' Lol, defiant, crammed the remains of Jo's bun into her mouth. 'My mum –' she swallowed – 'says it's very sexist for women always to be worrying about their figures and whether they appeal to men.'

'Well – yes.' If you put it like that, then Jo supposed it was rather sexist.

'My mum says people should like you for what you are, not for what you look like.'

'Mm . . .' Jo was doubtful. It sounded all right, but she couldn't help feeling that if Lol weren't so huge and enormous it would make her a happier sort of person, and that being a happier sort of person would make her a nicer sort of person, and then perhaps other people wouldn't keep ganging up on her and calling her names and threatening to punch her face in. Unfortunately, she couldn't think of any way of saying it without sounding rude and hurtful.

'In some places,' said Lol, 'they think that fat people are beautiful and that skinny ones are ugly. It all depends where you live.'

'Yes, I can see that,' said Jo. She could see that it was just as rotten for thin people in fat societies as for fat people in thin ones, and that it was just Lol's hard luck if she had been born into a thin one. On the other hand you couldn't *make* people suddenly start thinking that fat (or thin) was beautiful, any more than you could make them start thinking that cross-eyes or knock-knees were beautiful. The thing was, if you had cross-eyes or knock-knees you got something done about it.

She pointed this out to Lol, but Lol only licked bits of bun off her fingers and said that knock-knees and cross-eyes were different.

'If you've got knock-knees you can't walk properly, and if you've got cross-eyes you can't see properly.'

'Yes, but if you're –' Jo broke off, confused. She couldn't bring herself to say 'fat': it sounded so horribly personal – 'if you're *overweight*,' she said, 'it means you can't run properly, and then f'r instance you get stuck as goalkeeper all the time.' And Lol *had* complained to Miss Dysart and Miss Dysart had *told* her she ought to lose weight.

'I don't care!' Lol pushed her hair back over her ears. She had pretty hair, long and silvery with natural waves. 'Hockey's stupid anyway. And if I'm going to be a singer –'

'*Are* you?' said Jo.

'I haven't decided yet. But I might be. There's this man who comes into our restaurant who's a music teacher. He says I ought to have my voice trained.'

'What does Mrs Elliott say?'

'She says I ought, too. She says I've got one of the best voices in the school. I did the audition yesterday, for *Ballet Shoes*, and she said, "Thank you very much, Laurel. That was excellent. I think I can guarantee you'll be getting the part."'

'*The* part?'

'Posy,' said Lol.

Jo frowned. She couldn't *believe* Mrs Elliott would cast Lol in the part of Posy.

'You see, it doesn't matter,' said Lol, 'with singers. It doesn't matter if they're a bit bigger than other people. If they weren't big they wouldn't be able to sing. All the best singers are big. Opera singers, that is. That's why sometimes you get these fat ladies singing about how they're fading away . . . it doesn't *matter*. 'Cause it's art.'

'I see,' said Jo.

She only hoped Lol wasn't going to be disappointed.

8

'Caesar adsum jam for tea
Pliny aderat
Caesar was sick in omnibus
And Pliny in his hat.

'There!' Bozzy slapped her rough book triumphantly on to the table. Her face was flushed with her own success. 'What did you think of that?'

There was a long silence. It was Thursday evening and Barge had invited the rest of the gang round to her place for tea and to make a progress report on their contributions to the school magazine.

Bozzy was the only one who had actually completed anything. Fij had written a couple of lines and got stuck, Barge was still wrestling with the weighty problem of 'how to begin', and Jo, to her shame, still hadn't thought of anything. Somehow, what with hockey and gym and going to the Club, not to mention mountainous great hoards of homework, there just hadn't been the time.

'*Well*?' said Bozzy, growing impatient. 'What did you think of it?'

Fij cleared her throat. 'What is it supposed to be? Exactly?'

'It's a poem!' said Bozzy. 'In Latin,' she added.

'*Latin*?' Barge, never a great respecter of other people's feelings, gave a loud pig-like snort. 'News to me,' she said. 'If that's Latin, I'm a Chinese tea-pot!'

'Part Latin,' said Bozzy.

'I think it's rather clever,' said Jo. 'It's like a sort of . . . sort of franglais.'

'Do what?' said Fij.

'Like when people talk in a mixture of English and French and call it franglais.'

'Oh,' said Barge. 'Do they?'

'Well, some do.'

'First I heard of it.'

Barge was plainly sceptical. In general, anything she hadn't heard of didn't exist.

'My dad got a book of it for Christmas,' said Jo. 'Some of it's quite funny.'

'Oh,' said Barge. 'Is it?'

'Like what? For instance?'

'Well, like saying someone has their pantalon in a twist, or that – that someone's *un pain dans le bum* or –'

Barge waited.

'Yes, well . . . I mean,' said Jo, 'it is *quite* funny.'

'Yes, it is,' said Bozzy, giving a little snigger. 'Pain dans le bum . . . tee hee!'

Barge squashed her with a stare.

'Anyway,' said Jo, 'I think Bozzy's poem is quite funny. Actually.'

'Thank you,' said Bozzy. 'I'm glad someone round here has enough culture to appreciate the higher things of life.'

'Did you write it yourself?' said Jo.

'Well – yes. In a manner of speaking. I mean –' Bozzy

turned suddenly coy. 'It all depends,' she said, 'how one chooses to look at it.'

'That means *no*,' said Barge, 'in a word . . . she didn't.'

'I did in a way.'

'Oh, yes?' said Barge.

'What sort of way?' Fij was always prepared to give people the benefit of the doubt.

'In a collecting sort of way. Like when people go out,' said Bozzy, 'and collect folk songs and that. I went out and collected this.'

'Went out where? Exactly?'

'Oh! Round and about.'

Barge turned to the others. 'She pinched it off Roy, I bet.'

Bozzy's face flushed: Roy was her elder brother. 'I didn't *pinch* if off him, I *collected* it from him. There is a difference.'

'Oh,' said Barge. 'Is there?'

'Yes, there jolly well is! You ask people like . . . like Vaughan Williams!' They had done Vaughan Williams in music the other day. 'Going round collecting all those folk songs off of people. I bet he'd be jolly happy to hear he'd pinched them. Surprised they didn't put him in prison . . . imagine getting to be famous,' gurgled Bozzy, 'for going out pinching songs off of people!'

'At least he didn't pretend he'd written them. In any case,' said Barge, 'Vaughan Williams is dead.'

'So what?'

'So you're still alive,' pointed out Barge. 'You could get done for it.'

Bozzy looked uncomfortable. 'Not if I put *collected*

by. That would be all right, wouldn't it?' She turned, anxiously, to Jo. 'I'm only thinking of the House,' she said, '*I* wouldn't mind if they published it anonymously. It's the points I'm thinking of. And anyway –' struck by a sudden thought she turned back, venomously, to Barge. 'What about you?'

'I.' said Barge, loftily, 'am toying with my first line . . . *To be or not to be* –'

'Well!' spluttered Bozzy. 'That's original!'

Barge glared. '*To be or not to be, that is what I ask myself*.'

'So profound!' sighed Fij.

'What's more to the point,' said Bozzy, 'is what does she *answer* herself?'

'Well, I don't know yet, do I?' There was a hint of irritation in Barge's voice. 'That's as far as I've got.'

Bozzy sniffed.

'You can't rush these things,' said Fij. 'You have to wait for inspiration.'

'Which means, I take it,' said Barge, 'that you are still waiting?'

'As a matter of fact –' Fij spoke eagerly – 'what I'm waiting for is *suggestions* . . . I got as far as line three and then I sort of ran out of ideas. Shall I read you what I've done?'

'Yes, do,' said Jo, cosily. With any luck, by the time Fij had read her three lines and they had all made suggestions for the next three, it would be nine o'clock and Jo's dad would be arriving to pick her up, thus sparing her the embarrassment of having to confess that she had not so far written anything at all.

'Right,' said Fij. 'This is it.' Her face took on a soulful

aspect, as befitted a poetry reading. 'Are you ready?' They nodded. Jo sat on her hands on the edge of Barge's bed, Barge sat cross-legged on the floor, Bozzy was perched on an upturned wastepaper basket. Fij stood in the centre of the carpet, eyes upraised to heaven.

'*O to be in Petersham*,' intoned Fij, in a voice throbbing with significance, '*now that winter's here*,

'*In the town of Petersham, where all is cold and drear.*

'*Walking down the High Street* –' She stopped.

'Is that it?' said Barge.

'Well, it's as far as I've got at this moment.'

'It's jolly good,' said Jo. It sounded a bit like a poem they had read recently in English – *O to be in England, now that April's here* – but it would have seemed churlish to say so.

'Do you like it?' said Fij. 'It came to me in the bath – I just dashed it off. But now I've got stuck. "Walking down the High Street" –'

Silence, while they considered it.

'*I* know!' said Barge. *Walking down the High Street, full of chips and beer.*'

Fij looked pained. 'I am attempting,' she said, 'to write a lyric verse.'

'Oh! Pardon me, I'm sure,' said Barge. 'If we're going to be all *artistic* –'

'Well, but I don't want to write about *drunks*, said Fij.

'How about this?' Jo rocked forward on her hands. '*Walking down the High Street, full of slush and mud* –'

'Yes?'

Jo rocked, thinking of a rhyme. '*Walking down the High Street, full of slush and mud*,

'*When somewhere up above you, there comes this fearsome thud.*'

'That's *good*!' Bozzy gazed admiringly upon Jo. 'That's class, that is. Imagine being able to write poetry just like that!'

'So if Jam's so awfully clever at writing poetry,' said Barge, 'why don't we hear *her* contribution?'

'Oh, but we haven't finished O to be in England, I mean Petersham,' babbled Jo.

'I'm sure Fij is quite capable of finishing it on her own, now that you have done a whole two lines for her. And if we don't get a move on,' said Barge, 'it'll be too late.'

Jo took a breath. 'Yes. Well. The awful thing is, I've – I've gone and left mine at home!'

'So what is it about? You can surely tell us what it's about?'

'Um. Well. It's about a – um – a – a dinosaur,' said Jo. 'Living in a garden shed.'

'A dinosaur living in a garden shed?'

'Yes, and it – it goes and lays this egg in a – flower pot and they all wonder what is it and –'

'Who all wonders what it is?'

'The – um – the people. The people that own the shed. Because the dinosaur's gone away and left it. So they plant it in the flower pot – the egg, I mean – and um – well! That's as far as I've got.'

'And quite far enough,' said Barge, 'if you ask me. Whoever heard of dinosaurs living in garden sheds?'

'Wouldn't they be rather large?' wondered Fij.

'Not this one. This one's a *miniature* dinosaur.'

'I think it's brilliant,' said Bozzy, loyally. 'Absolutely brilliant! I can't wait to read it.'

Jo forced a smile. Really, she thought, I seem to do nothing these days except tell lies.

* * *

In the car on the way home her dad said, 'By the way, there was a telephone call for you while you were out.'

'For me?'

'Yes, but don't ask me who it was because I don't know. Your mother took the call.'

'Was it –' Jo tried, unsuccessfully, to ask the question without bringing a blush to her cheek. 'Was it a boy or a girl?'

'Oh, *ho!*' said her father. 'Expecting *boys* to ring us now, are we?'

'Not really.' Jo turned, carelessly, to look out of the window. 'It could be anybody.'

Or it could be Robbie. Ringing to check that she was going to be at the Club tomorrow. *On her own.* She was hoping that after last Friday's experience Lol wouldn't feel like going any more. She hadn't said anything about it, but then Jo hadn't seen much of her this week. Lol had taken to hanging around with a strange, wizened, pokey-nosed person called Jasmine French from Class 2. According to Fij, Jasmine French was completely mad.

'Mad but brilliant, if you know what I mean . . . I think she's probably a genius. Geniuses are always a bit loopy, aren't they?'

It would take a genius, Jo reckoned, to cope with Big Lol. Jasmine French sounded just right.

The first thing her dad said when they arrived home was, 'This young lady wants to know whether that was her boyfriend on the phone!' There were times when her dad really was *quite* unspeakable. If Tom had been there (which fortunately he wasn't) she would never have heard the end of it.

After her mother had said 'What boyfriend?' and her

dad had jocularly relayed the question – 'What boy-friend?' – and Jo had hotly and angrily denied having any boyfriend, her mother said, 'Actually it was Laurel. She sounded rather upset about something. I said you'd ring her.'

Bother. She was sick of Lol being upset about things. She was sick of having to listen while she whinged.

'You'd better go and do it straight away,' said Mrs Jameson, 'before it gets too late.'

She didn't want to do it straight away. She didn't want to do it at all. She wanted to go upstairs and write her poem about a dinosaur for the school magazine.

'Go on,' said her mother. 'Go and get it over with.'

'Do I have to? said Jo.

'Yes, you do! I told her you would.'

Jo heaved a loud sigh, full of suffering and being put-upon. Dutifully she trailed out to the hall and dialled Lol's number, only to find it engaged. She went back to the sitting-room for five minutes to watch television, then went back out and dialled again: still engaged. Good! Quickly, before whoever it was who was talking could stop talking and leave the line free, she scampered upstairs. No one could say she hadn't tried.

Next day, Lol wasn't in school. Jo's first feeling was one of relief – if Lol were off sick, then surely she wouldn't be coming to the Club tonight?

Her second feeling was one of slight guilt, because of not having rung. She *could* have tried again – but then Andy had been on the phone, having a heart-to-heart with his latest girlfriend, and Andy's heart-to-hearts, unless Mr Jameson came roaring out to put a stop to them, were liable to go one for an hour or more. As it happened, last night had been one of the occasions when Mr Jameson had come roaring out to put a stop, but by then Jo had already gone to bed. After all, *she* wasn't to have known. She might have had to stay awake till midnight.

When she told Fij, Fij said, 'Oh, the Lollipop's always getting upset! Then she says she's not well and her mum lets her stay home. Anyway, what's she ringing you for?'

Well, exactly, thought Jo; what was Lol ringing *her* for?

Later in the day, studying the notice-board in search of interesting notices, Jo came across the cast list for *Ballet Shoes*. The part of Posy had been given to Jasmine French: Lol was down as the old nurse, Nana. Now she understood what the problem was. Lol had been so certain of getting Posy! Jo had tried to warn her, but she wouldn't listen.

'Hello, there! Thinking of trying for the choir again?'

Jo spun round. Mrs Elliott, the music teacher, had come up behind her and was leaning across to pin another notice on the board. The notice said: THE JUNIOR CHOIR STILL HAS VACANCIES. ANYONE INTERESTED PLEASE SIGN BELOW.

Jo grinned. She had a good relationship with Mrs Elliott in spite of being almost totally unmusical.

'Shouldn't think there's much point,' she said. 'Not unless you're looking for people that are tone deaf.'

'Oh, come! I wouldn't say you're as bad as that. Pretty chronic, mind you . . . but what's the odd sharp or flat between friends? Are you looking at my cast list? What do you think of it?'

'I was just wondering,' said Jo, 'about Laurel.'

'Laurel? What about Laurel?'

'She really thought you'd promised her the part,' said Jo. It would be too awful if Mrs Elliott *had* promised her, and then changed her mind.

'I promised her *a* part,' said Mrs Elliott. 'And as you can see, she's got one. Was she expecting something different?'

'She really thought you'd promised her the part of Posy.'

'Posy?' Mrs Elliott sounded startled. 'Oh, but she's quite wrong for Posy! Posy's the ballet dancer.'

'Yes, I know. I did tell her. But she really thought – she thought it didn't matter. Not with singers.'

'Thought what didn't matter?'

'Well, if they were a bit sort of – big,' said Jo.

'It mightn't matter so much in grand opera,' said Mrs Elliott, 'but we're not aiming quite that high. What we're doing is a musical. I'm not saying the singing isn't important, because it is. Of course it is! But it's equally important that we have characters who look right for the part.'

'Yes,' said Jo. *She* could see that; why couldn't Lol?

'If it's any consolation,' said Mrs Elliott, 'you can tell her that she's one of the few people with a strong enough voice to be cast as an adult.'

'It it's any consolation,' said Jo, 'Mrs Elliott said you were one of the few people with a strong enough voice to be cast as an adult.'

From the way Lol continued sobbing at the other end of the telephone it obviously wasn't any consolation at all.

'She promised me,' blubbed Lol. 'She promised me the part!'

Patiently, for the second time, Jo explained: 'She promised you *a* part.'

'*The* part!'

Jo held the receiver away from her ear.

'What's the matter?' said Mrs Jameson, coming into the hall. 'Is that Laurel?' She took the telephone away from Jo. 'Hello, Laurel! This is Jo's mum. How are you? – Really? Oh, dear! Well, never mind, these things happen. Try not to take it too much to heart – after all, you have got a part. I expect there are loads of people who haven't got anything. And you're still only in your first year. Has anyone else from the first year got anything? No? Well, there you are, then! You ought to be celebrating! Are you going along to the Youth Club tonight?'

'*No*!' Jo mouthed it, desperately, at her mother. Mrs Jameson appeared not to notice.

'Why not? It would do you good. Take your mind off things. You go away and put something nice on and come straight round. I'll make sure the others wait for you.'

'*Mum*!' Jo glared accusingly at her mother as she put the receiver down. 'What did you go and do that for?'

'Don't be angry.' said Mrs Jameson. 'I felt sorry for her.'

Feeling sorry for Lol, thought Jo, sourly, was beginning to be an occupational hazard in her family.

9

Jo's evening at the Youth Club was ruined. Robbie was there, but so was Lol. Lol stuck like a leech from start to finish; there was simply no shifting her. Jo couldn't even get rid of her by going to play handball because it was what Mrs Barlow called a 'structured evening'. She had arranged a quiz and wanted to know if it was to be 'Boys against Girls, or would you rather pick sides?'

Most of the girls wanted boys against girls, but the boys (terrified, no doubt, of being thrashed, as they had been last time) clamoured for picking sides. As usual, it was the boys who got their own way. With yobs like Tom and his mates shouting their heads off, Jo supposed it was difficult to ignore them. For once, though, she didn't really mind: mixed teams meant she stood a chance of being with Robbie.

'All right!' said Mrs Barlow. 'Let's have . . . you! Nadia. And . . . you! Laurel, isn't it? You two come out here and choose.'

Nadge chose first: she chose Lee Powell, who was her best friend. Lol chose Jo. Nadge chose Tom (she had obviously forgiven him for deserting her, last term – Jo wouldn't have done) and Lol chose Matty.

'You ought to choose a boy next,' whispered Jo. 'Choose Robbie.'

Lol said, 'I don't want any boys.'

'You'll have to have *some*.'

Lol could be stubborn. She waited until the very end, when there were only boys left, and even then she didn't choose Robbie. Poor Robbie stood there, growing redder and redder because of the shame of being overlooked. Nadge kept shooting apologetic glances at Jo: *she* knew they wanted to be together. She would have picked Robbie ages ago, if it hadn't been for that.

Now there were only three boys left: a boy in a red sweater, a boy who kept picking his nose, and Robbie. Jo hissed, '*Choose Robbie*!'

'Him,' said Lol, pointing at the boy in the red sweater.

Nadge, with a last apologetic glance at Jo, finally took Robbie, leaving the horrible disgusting nose-picker for Lol. Jo couldn't blame Nadge. She had given Lol every opportunity, and who would want a nose-picker when they could have beautiful Robbie? As he moved across to sit with Nadge and her team, Robbie sent Jo a look of long reproach. In spite of her denials, he still believed that Lol was her friend.

'I hate her!' thought Jo. 'I hate her!'

Afterwards (when Nadge's team had thrashed Lol's by thirty-six points to fourteen) Robbie went off in a huddle with Tom and Keith Baxter. He didn't even look in Jo's direction. He was obviously hurt and angry and thought that it was Jo's fault he had been left till almost last.

Jo, all alone with Lol in the middle of the room, felt abandoned and hard-done-by. She felt that she would like to burst into tears. She knew, of course, that she mustn't – to cry in public was terribly shaming – but the

90

effort of keeping them back made her face go all red and her eyes all hot and prickly.

She heard Lol's voice in her ear: '. . . those horrible girls from Woodside. My mum said if they come here again I'm to report them. She says girls like that deserve punishing. I told you one of their mothers was a thief, didn't I? I told you –'

If she doesn't be quiet, thought Jo, I shall scream. She saw Jool and Matty, drinking Coke together. She saw Nadge and Lee Powell playing table tennis. She looked across at Robbie, willing him to turn his head, but he steadfastly refused to do so.

At her side, Lol went on whingeing: '. . . Jasmine French. She can't even *sing*. It's favouritism, that's all it is. Just because she takes private lessons out of school. It's not fair, people taking private lessons. Not from one of the teachers. It colours their judgement; that's what my mum says. She says if it hadn't been for Jasmine French being one of Mrs Elliott's private pupils I'd have got the part. Sh –'

'Oh, shut up!' Jo turned on her, viciously. 'I'm sick of hearing you moan all the time! The reason you didn't get the part is that you're just too *fat*!'

Jo stormed off, across the hall. To her fury, Lol followed her.

'Where are you going?'

'I'm going home!'

'You can't go home, my dad's coming to pick us up!'

'Well, I don't care,' said Jo. 'I'm going!'

Saturday was miserable. In the morning Jo went to the library by herself (to get out some books about dinosaurs) and bumped into Gerry Stubbs, who said she'd just completed an article on Roman burial mounds for the school mag.

'Roman burial mounds,' said Jo. 'Well, yes! My goodness. That does sound interesting.'

'I think so,' said Gerry. 'At least it will raise the tone a bit . . . they must grow so tired of members of the first year constantly submitting their potty little poems.'

'Bozzy has written a poem,' said Jo. 'In *Latin*.'

That should give Gerry something to think about. Her and her Roman burial mounds! Jo took out two books about dinosaurs and one about a girl who defeated all the odds to become an Olympic gold medallist at ice skating (Jo liked books about people who defeated all the odds, they made some of her own private fantasies, such as achieving international stardom as a gymnast, seem a bit more hopeful) and went home to write her potty little poem.

Unfortunately, the potty little poem didn't get very far. It stopped, in fact, after the first few lines.

Once upon a time
A dinosaur (since she had *said* she was writing a
    poem about a dinosaur, she felt duty bound to
    write one)
Laid its egg
In a pot
In a shed
The biggest egg
You ever saw
As befits
A dinosaur.

It was only then that she remembered: it was supposed to be a miniature dinosaur. A large dinosaur wouldn't even be able to get into a shed in the first place.

Jo sighed. She crossed out the last four lines and tried to think of a rhyme for shed. In her rough book she wrote 'Bed, dead, fed, head, led, red, said, wed'. Then she stopped and nibbled the end of her pen and chewed at a piece of her hair and thought all over again about last night at the Youth Club . . . Robbie deliberately ignoring her, and her marching out and arriving home early, and her mum asking awkward questions and Jo having to lie (*again*) and say she had a headache, and then Tom getting back and blowing it all, 'You didn't half give old Fatso what-for!' and her mum, naturally, wanting to know what had happened, and Tom going and telling her, in quite unnecessary detail (Jo hadn't realised her voice had carried all across the hall), and her mum getting mad, and Jo screeching and Tom bellowing and her mum telling them that they were 'ruddy rotten brats, the pair of you' and Jo being quite unable to explain about Robbie, and how Lol was ruining her life.

It had all been quite horrible and today didn't look as though it were going to be much better. Life was just so unfair.

Then at six o'clock that evening the telephone rang and it was Robbie – 'your mythical boyfriend,' said her dad, handing her the receiver – and suddenly everything was wonderful again. Robbie hadn't been deliberately ignoring her at all, he'd thought *she* was deliberately ignoring *him*. He had spent all night worrying about it and trying to pluck up the courage to ring her.

'I spent all night worrying, too,' said Jo.

'I really thought I'd done something,' said Robbie.

'I thought *I*'d done something . . . I told Lol to pick you, but she's so mean at times. She wouldn't do it, just to spite me. I knew you'd think it was me.'

'I thought it was 'cause you were mad at me.'

'*No*,' said Jo. 'It was Lol.'

There was a pause. Jo crinkled the telephone wire round her fingers and curled up her toes in her shoes.

'Actually,' she said, 'I was going to ask you something.'

'What?' said Robbie.

'I was going to ask you, when I have my birthday party at half-term, would you like to come?'

'Yes, please,' said Robbie.

Jo said that she would give Tom a proper invitation to take in to school with him on Monday. 'But you don't have to bother RSVP-ing if you don't want to.'

Robbie said that of course he would RSVP: 'It would be rude if I didn't.'

Joe replaced the receiver on its rest and bounced two at a time up the stairs to her room. Robbie was coming to her party! It made the day perfect.

She still wasn't able to get any further with her poem about the dinosaur, but maybe on Sunday something would come to her.

What came to her on Sunday, as it had on the last two Sundays, was the lumbering form of Big Lol. Jo could have screamed. She looked out of the window and there it was, humping itself up the garden path. Fortunately Jool and Matty weren't there to say 'I told you so' but still Jo felt like screaming. She felt like screaming 'Go away and leave me alone!' She was beginning to sympathise with Gerry Stubbs, who in the end had had to resort to being brutal and telling her to push off.

Tom came galloping up the stairs, his face all a-beam like a gleeful garden gnome, to give her the news: 'Fatso's here!'

If she starts moaning, thought Jo, I shall go mad.

For once, it seemed, the Lollipop hadn't come to moan; she was, for the Lollipop, quite humble. To begin with she apologised to Jo for not having picked Robbie for the team – 'I didn't know he was your boyfriend.'

Jo blushed, instantly disarmed. 'He's not exactly my *boyfriend*. I just thought it would be good to have him on our side.'

'I was trying not to have any boys on our side. I don't like boys. I think they're stupid.'

'Some are,' agreed Jo, thinking of Tom and Keith Baxter. 'Some are all right.'

'I haven't met any that are all right. Whenever I meet them they're just horrible.'

Jo didn't know what to say to that.

'It's because I'm fat.' said Lol. 'They think because you're fat you haven't got feelings the same as other people. My mum says take no notice of them, but I can't. I really hate it when people are unkind. It really upsets me.'

Jo had a moment of fellow feeling. It wasn't easy, taking no notice of boys when they set out to tease you or make you embarrassed. She knew that from living with Tom.

'I expect you think I ought to lose weight,' said Lol.

'Um – well –' Jo was flustered. What was she supposed to say to that? Last time she had mentioned losing weight Lol had strenuously denied that she needed to. She had as good as accused Jo of being sexist.

'It's all right,' said Lol. 'You can say if you do.'

'Well, I do think it would be *better*,' said Jo. 'I mean, I'm sure you'd *feel* better. And it would be loads healthier.' (Everyone said it wasn't good for you, being overweight.) 'And although it's quite true, what you said before, about people liking you for what you are and not for what you look like, it does at least help if you look *reasonably* the same as everyone else and don't sort of – sort of stand out. In the wrong sort of way. If you know what I mean? And just think,' urged Jo, growing enthusiastic at the prospect of Lol actually shedding a couple of stone and Jo being the one who had helped her do it, 'think of all the *clothes* you could wear!' An idea suddenly came to her. 'I could write a poem for the school magazine!

> *I look in the mirror, and what do I see?*
> *A shadow of the former me . . .*

'I could write it,' said Jo, 'and you could do the illustrations. We could call it "Before and After."'

'But the magazine contributions have to be in by the end of term,' said Lol.

'Well, that's weeks away! It gives us loads of time.'

'I can't get thin by the end of term!'

'You could try. If you got going straight away –'

'How?'

'Well . . . on a diet, I suppose.'

'Would you go on a diet with me?'

'Me?' Jo practically was on a diet already, what with

96

all the things she didn't like or couldn't stand or made her feel sick.

'I could do it better if it were both of us. I've already tried on my own,' said Lol. 'It doesn't work. If you did it with me I might be able to stick to it.'

Jo pulled a strand of hair into her mouth and chewed at it. She didn't know what her mum would say, if she were to announce that she was going on a diet. She already complained enough as it was about Jo not eating properly.

'You can't say you don't *need* to,' said Lol. 'Everybody's got *some* fat they can lose.' She reached out and pinched Jo's waist, painfully, between finger and thumb. 'Look!'

Jo looked. She felt where Lol was pinching her, and it was quite true, there was some fat there. Not a great deal, but undeniably some.

'If you lost that,' said Lol, cunningly, 'you'd be slim as Claire.'

It was the wrong thing to have said: Jo didn't like to think back and remember the follies of last term. (She had actually, for a short while, had dreams of becoming a ballet dancer herself.) She tossed her head.

'I don't care about being as slim as Claire!'

'All right, then,' said Lol. 'I don't care, either.'

She looked at Jo, challengingly. She seemed to be saying, it's up to you . . . it's your responsibility. Either you help me and I lose weight, or you refuse to help me and I just go on getting fatter and fatter and miserabler and miserabler.

Jo rubbed at her waist, where Lol had pinched it. 'My mum would go spare.'

'So would mine,' said Lol.

She really didn't see why Lol's mum should go spare. You'd think Lol's mum would be only too *glad* if her daughter started consuming less.

'She thinks it's sexist,' said Lol. 'And then she keeps giving me all these things she's made, and if I say I don't want them she gets all upset and says she's made them specially, and then my dad gets upset 'cause she's upset, and then I get upset; and I just can't manage by myself. I just start eating again. I just do it to stop them being upset. You don't know what it's like,' said Lol, 'when my dad gets upset. It makes me feel awful. That's why I've got to have someone else to do it with me, to give me encouragement.'

Jo sighed. 'Oh, all right,' she said. She always found it difficult to resist appeals. 'But if we do it we've got to do it properly.'

'I'll do it properly!'

'There won't have to be any cheating, or anything.'

'I won't cheat! I promise! But one thing *you've* got to promise,' said Lol.

'What?'

'You've got to promise to keep it a secret. Even from Matty. Even from Fij. You've got to promise!'

'I promise,' said Jo.

'You won't tell *anyone*?'

'I won't tell anyone.'

'Not even Robbie?'

Why on earth should she think that Robbie would be interested?

'I told you,' said Jo. 'I *promised*.'

'Swear a solemn oath,' said Lol. 'Swear you'll do it

with me and swear you won't tell a single soul.'

Jo sighed. 'All right,' she said. 'I swear.'

10

'Crisps –'

Jo flipped through the pages of her new *Count Your Calories* book. She had bought the book (secretly) on her way home from school one evening, when Matty had had to stay late for a choir practice. If a thing's worth doing, it's worth doing properly; that was what her dad always said, and Jo agreed with him. She always threw herself into things wholeheartedly. (Sometimes a bit too wholeheartedly, like the time she had taken up gardening and dug up a whole flowerbed before anyone could stop her. But that had been when she was only nine years old: she had more sense now.)

'*Crisps, potato – see potato crisps*. And under potato crisps . . . *pork pie, porridge, port wine . . . potato crisps! ONE HUNDRED AND FIFTY-ONE CALORIES!*'

'Is that a lot?' said Lol.

'Yes, it jolly well is a lot!'

'But I need 2,300 calories a day!' wailed Lol. 'I looked it up in my mum's diet book . . . it said, "recommended daily intake for normal eleven-year-old, 2,300 calories".'

Jo resisted the temptation to point out that Lol was not a normal eleven-year-old, but an extremely fat and fast getting even fatter eleven-year-old. It may have been true, but it would have seemed too brutal.

She said, 'You're meant to be on a *diet*. Potato crisps are fattening. Write it down.' She pointed, sternly, at the notebook where Lol was supposed to be making lists of Things Not To Be Eaten.

Lol heaved a sigh. Obediently, she wrote 'Crisps, 151 calories'. She didn't look too happy about it. Jo wasn't that happy, either. Crisps were one of the few things she enjoyed.

'Potato baked in jacket is all right,' said Jo. 'That's only thirty. And potato boiled. Potato *boiled* is only twenty-two.'

'What about pizza?'

Jo flipped back a page. 'It says, *pizza, tomato and cheese* . . . sixty-eight. Pizza's not bad.' Except that Jo loathed it. What could she eat that she didn't loath? 'Apples, oranges, radishes . . . radishes are good! You can eat three radishes for only four calories. And celery . . . *celery fresh raw*. That's only *two* calories.'

'What about bananas?'

'Bananas . . . *fresh peeled, twenty-two*.'

'Good!' Lol's face brightened. 'So I can eat bananas.'

'Well, but not too many of them,' said Jo. 'When it says twenty-two it means twenty-two per *ounce*. And I bet if you weighed a banana –' especially some of the whopping great jobs that Lol munched her way through – 'I bet it would weigh at least six ounces. That brings it up to –' she did some quick sums on her fingers – 'that brings it up to a hundred and thirty-two!'

'Yes, but you've got to eat *something*,' said Lol.

'Beans – sprouts – salad –'

'You can't just eat beans and sprouts and salad!'

'No, but you've got to cut out the fattening stuff – at

101

least, you have if you want to lose weight. And you *do* want to lose weight,' said Jo, 'don't you?'

Lol looked down at her list. She heaved a sad sigh. 'I suppose so.'

'Well, you do,' said Jo, ''cause you said you did. And you made a *promise*. What we'll do, we'll go and weigh ourselves and see what we weigh, then we'll make a note of it and we'll write down everything we eat, every day for a whole week, and then we'll weigh ourselves again and see if we've lost anything. So let's go and do that,' said Jo, 'and then we'll feel that we've started.'

They went into the bathroom and locked the door.

'We'll have to take our clothes off,' said Jo. 'We've got to do it properly.'

'I'll just take my jeans off,' said Lol. 'The jumper doesn't weigh anything.'

'Actually it probably does,' said Jo, but she didn't insist. She was remembering what her mother had said about how embarrassing it must be for someone like Lol having to strip off in communal changing rooms in front of everyone. Give it a few weeks, thought Jo, and the Lollipop would strip off in front of anybody – and it would be all thanks to Jo! The spirit of the crusader came upon her. She wasn't going to rest till Lol had lost at least two stone. *At least*.

Not eating fattening food, Jo discovered, was rather like saving money. It might sound dismal to begin with – because after all a bag of crisps was far tastier than a plateful of lettuce leaves, just as spending your pocket money on books and records was far more fun than putting it through a hole in a china pig – but once you'd actually got going, it was surprising how fast it caught hold of you.

'Pardon me for asking,' said Barge, one lunch time, as she walloped her way through a vast mound of spaghetti, 'I don't mean to be personal but have you by any chance become a Muslim?'

'Me?' said Jo. 'No, why?'

'Well, I just thought you might be, since you seem to be perpetually fasting.'

Bozzy leaned forward, contentiously. 'Why should that make her a Muslim?'

'Because we have Muslims living next door to us,' said Barge, 'and they fast.'

'So do hunger strikers.'

'Well, yes, that is true.'

'She could be on a hunger strike.'

They looked across at Jo.

'*Are* you on a hunger strike.'

'Not really,' said Jo, toying with a heap of baked beans which she had unwisely allowed one of the servers to dump on her plate. (She couldn't eat baked beans until she had checked in her calorie book and made sure they were permissible, and she couldn't check in her calorie book until she could get away somewhere private, like the lavatories.) 'I'm just trying to eat things that are healthy.'

'Well, it seems to me,' said Barge, 'that you are becoming decidedly peculiar.'

'People can eat what they want to eat,' objected Fij. 'There aren't any rules.'

'There may not be any rules, but there is such a thing as *normality*. I don't call it normal,' said Barge, 'to suck the inside out of a baked potato and pretend it's a meal.'

'The skin's all nobbly,' said Jo.

'And what about the baked beans? What's wrong with them?'

'I don't feel like baked beans.'

'Can I have them?' said Bozzy. She leaned forward and began scooping them off Jo's plate. Bozzy was rather like a human version of a dustbin. One way and another she probably ate as much as the Lollipop. It was one of life's unfairnesses that the Lollipop spread and Bozzy didn't. Of course Bozzy *was* very aggressive; it was possible she burnt most of it off.

'Well! All I can say,' said Barge, juggling with loops of spaghetti, 'is that you had better watch it or you'll find yourself going into a decline.'

'And if she does,' said Bozzy, 'we're not having Lol back.'

'Pity Lol doesn't go into a decline.'

'She couldn't,' said Bozzy, stuffing her mouth with baked beans. 'Not even if she starved for a year . . . she'd just live off her own fat.'

'Great gooey blancmange!'

Jo wished she could tell them of the efforts Lol was making. She knew that Lol *was* making them, because she saw her every day in the canteen. It wasn't a question of spying: Lol actually went out of her way to demonstrate how well she was sticking to the Not Eating rules. Whereas before she would pile her tray high with fish and chips and sticky cakes, she now pointedly walked past with a plate of salad and a yoghurt, or a piece of cheese-and-onion quiche and an orange. Jo felt quite proud of her. She felt as if she were a teacher and Lol was

104

her pupil. She knew now how Miss Lloyd must feel when someone turned in a specially good essay: rewarded for all the effort she had made.

On Sunday when Lol came round – Jo was resigned, by now, to seeing Lol on a Sunday – they compared their Eating Notes.

'I've eaten a bit more than you,' said Lol, 'but I couldn't *exist* on anything less. If I don't have a proper breakfast I just can't last out.'

'A proper breakfast is all right so long as it's not huge and fattening,' said Jo. 'For instance, fried bread –' the pages in her *Count Your Calories* book were becoming distinctly dog-eared – 'fried bread is *ONE HUNDRED AND FIFTY-EIGHT*!'

'I only had it once,' pleaded Lol.

'Well, you mustn't have it again. It's *very bad*.'

Lol looked crestfallen. 'I'll just have bacon and eggs in future.'

Jo hadn't the heart to tell her that bacon and eggs were almost – not quite, but *almost* – as bad as fried bread. It was easy for Jo. Eggs made her feel sick and she wouldn't eat bacon because of the poor pigs, and in any case she didn't really care for fried food, other than chips. She could see that for the Lollipop it might be asking rather a lot, that she should give up everything all at once. Little by little, thought Jo. Making progress was what mattered.

'Let's go and weigh ourselves again and see if we've lost anything.'

Jo, in spite of eating almost next to nothing, had only lost a pound: Lol had lost almost four.

'For that,' declared Jo, 'you should get a gold star!'

Lol beamed. 'We ought to have a points system . . . a gold star if you lose four pounds, a silver star if you lose two, and just an ordinary star if you lose one.'

'Yes, and a big black mark if you don't lose anything at all!' Lol was all flushed and confident, now she had shed a whole four pounds. What was more, she hadn't moaned once about anyone calling her names or being beastly to her.

'Now that you've got started,' said Jo, 'you'll find it gets easier and easier . . . next week you might even get a *super*star!'

'I don't know about next week.' Lol's face puckered slightly. Next week was half-term. 'We're going over to Italy to see my nan.'

'Well, you can still stick to your diet, can't you?' said Jo.

'I'll try to,' said Lol. 'I will, honestly . . . I will try. But you don't know my nan. She keeps cooking all this pasta and stuff. It's really, really fattening, and if I don't eat it she gets really hurt.'

Everyone made such a big thing about eating, thought Jo. It sometimes seemed to her that eating was really rather a nuisance. If she had her way there wouldn't be any food, just pills that you could swallow with a bit of water. Imagine the time it would save! All the shopping and the cooking and the washing-up. She'd suggested it once to Matty, but Matty had told her quite bluntly, 'You must be nuts! I *like* eating.'

That was the trouble: people were so gross when it came to their stomachs.

'I almost wish we weren't going on holiday,' said Lol.

'Yes, it is a pity, it means you'll miss my birthday party.'

Secretly Jo was glad that Lol was going to miss the party. She would have had to invite her because Mrs Jameson would have insisted, and anyway she would have felt mean if she hadn't, but Matty would have groaned and Jool would have said 'I told you so' and it would only have caused trouble with Barge and Bozzy. Now that Lol was out of the Gang they said they simply couldn't think why they had ever let her in in the first place.

'So *unsuitable* –'

'Not one of us at *all*.'

Even Fij agreed that Jo fitted in far better.

'Maybe,' said Lol, 'I could get Mum to let me stay behind. She might let me. I could stay with our friends that live over the road and then I'd be able to come.'

Jo lived in dread for the rest of the week. It wasn't till school broke up on Thursday that Lol, regretfully, informed her, 'Mum says I've got to go, I haven't seem my nan for over a year.' Jo felt so relieved that she gave Lol her copy of *Count Your Calories* (though it wasn't such a big sacrifice to make: she had looked at it so often she almost knew it off by heart).

The people Jo had invited to her party were: Fij, Barge and Bozzy: Matty and Jool: Nadge: Miles, Tom and Robbie. If it hadn't been for Robbie she wouldn't have let Tom come anywhere near. Last year, because Mrs Jameson had said that it didn't do to be sexist, she had invited not only Tom and Miles but some of Tom's horrible friends from school, including Keith Baxter. They had ruined every single game by their shouting and bad manners. Tom had broken one of Mrs Jameson's favourite ornaments (a green china horseshoe for putting flowers in, given to her by Jo) and Keith Baxter had stuck his elbow in a girl's eye and made her scream. This year, even Mrs Jameson had agreed that Jo could be sexist if she wanted.

'Perhaps,' Jo had ventured, thinking of Robbie, 'perhaps we ought to give them just one more chance?'

'That's very noble of you,' said her mother. 'But you don't have to if you don't want to. I should take great pleasure in informing Master Thomas that he's still too much of a barbarian for polite company.'

Jo had had to struggle really hard to find a convincing argument for Tom being given another chance.

'Maybe if we just had him and Miles and one other . . . maybe then he'd be a bit more civilised. 'Cause Miles is.'

'Oh, Miles is all right. I don't have any problem with Miles. It's your brother and his crew I'm thinking of.'

'It's that Keith,' said Jo. 'We won't have *him*.'

Surprisingly, Tom didn't raise too much of a protest at the omission of his supposed best friend. Jo had thought he would rage and sulk, because this time last year he and Keith Baxter had been inseparable. This year he seemed quite happy that it should just be him and Robbie; and of course Miles.

'So what sort of things do you want to eat?' said Mrs Jameson.

'Mm . . .' Jo crinkled her nose, thinking about it. 'We could have carrots and things, stuck on sticks . . . and *jellies* –'

'Jellies?' shouted Tom. That's kids' stuff!'

Yes, thought Jo, but it was very low in calories. It practically had none at all.

'Leave it to me,' said Mrs Jameson. 'I'll see what I can do.'

In the end there were bits of all sorts of things stuck on sticks; plus bowls of crisps and savoury strips; and lasagne and sausage rolls (made out of soya meat so that Jo could eat them without worrying about the poor pigs) and a special 'Jo sort of birthday cake'; plain sponge (because she couldn't stand currants and sultanas) with pink icing on the top.

'This is *brilliant*!' said Nadge, diving into the sausage rolls.

Jo also dived into the sausage rolls. It wasn't until she'd eaten her way, totally unthinkingly, through three and a half that she remembered about calories. Pastry must have simply oodles and *oodles*. Visions of Lol rose before her. She had given the Lollipop strict instructions not to gorge, and here was she doing exactly that very thing.

Guiltily, when no one was looking, she broke open the remains of the pastry case, separated it from the sausage and dropped it in her mother's rubber plant. She only hoped rubber plants didn't mind having pastry dropped into them. It would be terrible if it went and died because of having a pastry allergy.

When it came to birthday cake, Jo nobly helped herself to the smallest piece on the plate. She wasn't going to miss out on her own cake, not even for Lol, but at least she could exercise good manners and not automatically snatch at the biggest bit she could see (which was what Tom always did unless Mrs Jameson got at him first).

The cake was all gooey and gorgeous. There was butter icing in the middle, two centimetres thick, and a polished pink skating rink of ordinary icing on the top, decorated with little silver balls and chocolate drops. I am *gorging*, thought Jo. It was lovely. She could understand, now, how Lol presumably felt all of the time. She decided that what she would do, she would live on nothing but salad for the whole of next week to make up for it. (She would never be able to look Lol in the eye if she got on the scales and found she had actually grown *heavier*.)

Apart from trouble with calories, the party was a great success. Tom, without Keith Baxter to egg him on, behaved remarkably well. They played a few party games, such as Pass the Parcel and Musical Chairs, to please Jo's mum (because those were the games that she had played when she was a girl) but instead of bellowing 'That's kids' stuff!' and making his disgusting being-sick noises, Tom joined in without a murmur and even seemed to enjoy himself. At one point he crashed into Bozzy and sent her flying, and right at the end he bounced on to a chair so hard that he broke the back of it, but that was just excitement; not like last year when he had been rough and rude on purpose.

Robbie behaved like a dream. He had bought Jo a present – a china cat to go with her cat collection (how had he *known*? Had he asked Tom?) – he shook hands politely, like a grown-up, with Mrs Jameson, he didn't crash into anyone or break any chairs, and when they had forfeits and he had to 'stand up and do a dance with someone' he chose Jo.

Mrs Jameson said afterwards what a nice young man

110

he was. 'He's going to be a real heart-throb when he get older.'

'He's Jo's boyfriend,' said Tom.

'Shut up!' said Jo. 'He's not.'

'Don't lie! He is!'

'He's *not*!'

'Do you want me to tell him that?' said Tom.

Jo blushed.

'Well, if he is,' said Mrs Jameson, 'I think she's got very good taste.'

So there.

When Lol came round the following Sunday and they weighed themselves, Jo got a silver star: in spite of gorging on three and a half sausage rolls and a slice of birthday cake, she had still managed to lose almost two pounds. Lol on the other hand got a big black mark: not only had she not lost anything, she had actually gained.

'You haven't been sticking to your diet!' cried Jo.

'I couldn't help it, I told you,' babbled Lol, 'it's my nan, she's always cooking stuff, pasta and stuff, and if you don't eat it they all start getting at you – "what's the matter with you, why aren't you eating, you'll have to go and see the doctor, there must be something wrong with you . . ." you don't know what it's like,' said Lol, 'living with an Italian family. They're all fat, in Italy.'

Jo couldn't help feeling this was something of an exaggeration – they couldn't *all* be fat. What about Italian ballet dancers and Italian models and Italian athletes? But it was true that Lol's dad was rather on the large side, and she could quite see that being in someone else's house on holiday might present difficulties.

'In the circumstances,' she said sternly, sounding like Barge at her most Bargelike, 'I am prepared to overlook it – *just this once*. But now that you're back in England there is no excuse. I shall expect a marked improvement next week.'

'Oh, yes, there will be,' said Lol. 'There will be, I promise!'

'There'd better be,' said Jo. She didn't see why she should be expected to cut down on her own birthday cake if Lol were just going to go on gluttonising and getting fatter and fatter. 'I shall check your diet sheet,' said Jo, 'and make sure there's no more cheating!'

11

That Friday at the Youth Club they played rounders. Jo and Robbie were on the same side, but Jo wasn't feeling inspired and didn't play very well. She didn't score a single rounder and was one of the first to be out – caught by the Lollipop, of all people.

Nadge, of course, showed everybody up, just as she always did. Robbie said admiringly, 'She's really good isn't she?' and Jo was instantly filled with horrible pea-green jealousy. *She* was really good when she played properly.

She didn't know what the matter was, but everything seemed to be going wrong this second half of term. She had tried for the Under-13s hockey and had been put down as reserve, while both Fij and Barge had gained places. (And Nadge, needless to say.) Jo *knew* that she was better then either of them. Then in English Miss Lloyd had returned an essay marked C+ with the comment 'Way below your usual standard!'; and Mrs Stanley, in Maths, had accused her of 'simply not bothering to try', which was quite unfair because she *had* bothered. The reason she'd got everything wrong was that she simply hadn't been able to follow Mrs Stanley's explanations. When she offered this as an excuse, Mrs Stanley had snapped, 'You would have followed perfectly well if you'd only made a bit more of an effort!'

It wasn't like Mrs Stanley to snap; at any rate, not at Jo. She and Jo had always got on well; in spite of Jo not being mathematical. Jo couldn't understand it: the first half of term had gone so *well*. Now she couldn't even manage to score a rounder against a team which had people like Jool and the Lollipop on it.

To solace herself she went racing across to Lol and snatched a can of fizzy drink away from her.

'What are you *doing*?' Everyone knew that fizzy drinks were crammed full of calories. 'Honestly! I can't take my eyes off you for one second!'

Jo tossed the can contemptuously into the dustbin. Lol's eyes followed it.

'It was a diet drink,' she said. 'I chose it specially.'

It might have been a diet drink and she might have chosen it specially, but when she came round on Sunday and they shut themselves in the bathroom to weigh themselves, she hadn't lost a single ounce.

'This is *terrible*,' said Jo. Jo had lost another whole pound and could hardly pinch any flesh at all round her waist. 'I don't believe you've been trying!'

'I have!' said Lol. 'I have! Your scales must be wrong!'

'They're exactly the same scales we've always used.'

'Well, then, it's my jumper! I've got a different jumper!'

'I told you,' said Jo, 'you ought to strip off. And anyway I don't think it is your jumper . . . try taking it off and weighing yourself without it.'

Lol backed away. 'It's all right, I'll wear the other one again next week.'

'TAKE IT OFF!' roared Jo.

Reluctantly, Lol did so; even more reluctantly she

stepped on the scales. Jo looked, and could hardly believe it . . . even without the sweater Lol was a whole pound heavier than when they had started!

In vain did Lol protest that 'That quite often happens, you start to lose weight and then you put it on, it happens to loads of people, it's to do with your body chemistry, you have to put weight *on* before you can get rid of it, it's what's known as metabolism.'

'You mean it's what's known as *overeating*.'

'It's not overeating! I haven't eaten *anything*, hardly. I– '

Lol broke off as there came the sound of heavy hammering on the bathroom door, followed by Tom's voice: 'How much longer are you two going to be in there?'

'As long as it takes!' shrieked Jo.

'Why? What are you up to?'

'None of your business!'

'It is my business! I want to wash my hands!'

'That'd make a change!'

'*Let me in*!' bawled Tom.

'No! Go and wash them downstairs.'

'I don't want to wash them downstairs, I want to wash them in the bathroom!'

'Well, you'll just have to wait.'

'I'm going to count up to ten,' shouted Tom, 'and if you're not out by then I shall bash the door in!'

'Oh yeah?' said Jo.

Lol looked at her, nervously. She was already back inside the sweater. 'Oughtn't we to let him in?'

'When I feel like it,' said Jo. Just at the moment she wasn't feeling like it, she was feeling petty and provoking. She turned both taps full on and began running water, very noisily, into the washbasin. 'La de da di dum!' sang Jo, splashing her hands in the water.

Tom rattled the door handle, 'Let me in, you bitch!'

'Ho de ho di ha,' sang Jo, enjoying herself.

'Did you hear what he called you?' said Lol.

Tom had called her worse things than that in his time. Tom was a specialist in name-calling.

'I'm warning you!' bellowed Tom.

'Why? What are you going to do?'

'I'll bash the bloody door down!'

'Go on, then.'

Tom kicked, feebly, at the bottom of it. Jo's reflection in the mirror smirked happily at itself.

'Her mother's voice came up the stairs: 'Tom? What are you doing?'

'I want to wash my hands! They won't let me into the bathroom!'

'Who says we won't let you into the bathroom?' Jo flung open the door and swept regally out, followed by a cringing Lol. 'You only had to ask *nicely*.'

She felt better now that she had scored over Tom; less irritated with the world in general and with Lol in particular. More inclined to show patience and tolerance in the face of other's shortcomings. Lol needed to be *helped*, not harangued.

'Right,' said Jo. She closed her bedroom door and pushed a chair against it. (Tom didn't like being scored over: she would never put it past him to mount a surprise attack.) 'There's only one way to tackle this, and that is *scientifically*.'

Lol's eyes widened, apprehensively. For the first time Jo noticed that they really *were* blue, the same as

116

Robbie's – except that Robbie's were a deep, dark, indigo blue, like violets or pansies. Lol's were more like washed-out cotton frocks. But quite pretty, for all that.

'Let's compare Eating Notes.' Jo kept her Eating Notebook hidden away beneath the bottom of her wardrobe. To get at it she had to lie full length on the floor and slide her arm underneath. 'What we'll do; we'll see what we've both eaten and we'll add up all the calories and that'll tell us where you're going wrong. I'll make out a table . . . I'll put the days of the week across the top . . . then I'll put "Lol: Breakfast Dinner Tea Supper", then I'll put the same for me, then we'll add them up. So let's start on Monday. What did you have for breakfast on Monday?'

For breakfast on Monday Lol had had cereal, toast-and-honey and a cup of tea: Jo had had a glass of orange juice and an apple.

For lunch Lol had had curry and rice, and rhubarb crumble: Jo had had two pieces of Ryvita, one orange and a strawberry yoghurt.

For tea Lol claimed not to have had anything at all: Jo had had bread and butter and a banana.

For supper Lol had had minestrone soup and a slice of pizza, while Jo had had potato and sprouts, 'without gravy', and tinned peaches 'in juice not syrup'.

It wasn't really possible to work out the calories because, as Lol was quick to point out, 'You don't always know how many ounces you've eaten. But I haven't had *anything*, hardly, that's fattening. Not really, I haven't.'

When Jo looked at Lol's diet over the course of the week, this seemed on the whole to be true.

'So how come I'm losing weight and you're not?'

'It's my metabolism,' moaned Lol. 'Some people just can't lose weight no matter how little they eat.'

'I don't believe that,' said Jo. 'I think that's just an excuse.'

Lol sulked. 'Then you think of an explanation!'

'I'm thinking.'

'It's all right for you, you're naturally skinny.'

'But I wouldn't be skinny,' said Jo, 'if I pigged all the time.'

'I haven't pigged all the time! I haven't eaten a single thing that's on the List.'

'What about rhubarb crumble?'

'Rhubarb crumble isn't on the List!'

'It's a pudding,' said Jo. 'I haven't eaten *any* puddings, almost.'

'But I couldn't exist on what you eat!' wailed Lol. 'I'm built bigger than you are . . . my bones are bigger. I need more! If you look at those chart things they always say "Big Bones and Little Bones" . . . you've got little bones. It's not fair!' cried Lol. 'It's not fair getting mad at me!'

'I'm not getting mad at you,' said Jo. 'I'm trying to help. Perhaps what it is – perhaps if you just tried eating the same sort of things but a bit less . . . *that* wouldn't be too difficult, I shouldn't have thought. Would it?'

Lol sniffed, self-pityingly. 'I'm eating hardly anything as it is.'

'Well – but just a *spoon*ful less. You'd look really good,' said Jo, 'if you could just lose a couple of stones. You'd be every bit as pretty as Melanie, and maybe, if Jasmine French really isn't any use, Mrs Elliott might let you be Posy instead of her.' She couldn't in all honesty see Lol losing enough weight quickly enough to play the

118

part of a ballet dancer, but one had to offer some encouragement.

'What about that poem? said Lol.

'Which poem?'

'The one you were going to write about me . . . the before-and-after one. For the magazine.'

'Oh, yes! I'd forgotten that. And you were going to do the illustrations.'

'Have you written it yet?'

'No, but I will,' promised Jo. 'I'll write the poem if you'll keep on trying to lose weight.'

'I'm only going to keep on trying if you do,' said Lol. 'I can't do it by myself.'

Jo might have pointed out that there wasn't any reason for her to keep on trying – she had already *lost* weight – but that would have been discouraging.

'All right,' she said. 'We'll go on doing it, so long as you promise on your honour that you're not cheating.'

'I'm not!' cried Lol. 'Cross my heart and hope to die!'

That afternoon, Jo wrote her poem:

> *I look in the mirror and what do I see?*
> *A shadow of the former me.*
> *Where once upon a time I had*
> *A roll of fat for shoulder pad*
> *And big balloons for both my hips*
> *And bulbous blobs for fingertips*
> *And round my waist a blown up tyre*
> *(The sort that motorists admire)*
> *And calves that bulged and arms that billowed*
> *And at my rear a bottom pillowed*

I now behold with greatest glee
A poised and slimline slender me.

From gorging crisps and Coke and pasta
I learnt at last to shout out 'Basta!'
And turned to fruit and veg. instead,
To celery and wholemeal bread,
To apples, radishes and pears,
And running up and down the stairs
And being madly energetic
Instead of fat and apathetic.

And that is how I thus became
A rose by any other name.
A tiny captivating elf –
A shadow of my former self!

Jo was extremely proud of her poem (the longest one she had even written). She was particularly proud of the word 'basta'. She had heard Mr Bustamente shout it one day in the car, when they were going to the Youth Club and the Lollipop had kept biffing him about the head with her anorak.

'Basta!' he had shouted. 'Basta!'

Jo at first had thought he was being rude and shouting 'bastard', but it had turned out that 'basta' was Italian for 'enough'.

On Monday morning (carefully choosing a moment when Barge and Co. were not around) she gave a copy of the poem to Lol.

'There you are! Now you can do the illustrations.'

Unfortunately, Bozzy appeared before Lol had a chance to say what she thought of it. Jo shot back to her desk and watched, under cover of her desk lid, as Lol read the poem through. (She could see her lips moving as they shaped the words.) She waited, eagerly, for some sign of approval – a grin or nod at the very least. Instead, Lol's face turned slowly pink, and then radish-coloured. She put the poem away in her bag and didn't even look in Jo's direction.

She had lots of opportunities during the day to come up and tell Jo whether she had liked it or not, but she never bothered. Jo thought that was really ungracious. She had gone to all that effort to write an encouraging sort of poem – she had spent practically the whole of Sunday working on it – and Lol couldn't even take the trouble to come and thank her.

It was only later that it occurred to Jo that possibly Lol hadn't been too happy at having herself described as bulbous and billowing – *And round her waist a blown up tyre (The sort that motorists admire)*.

For a moment she felt stricken, because in the thrill of composition she had never stopped to consider that Lol's feelings might be hurt; but then she hardened her heart and thought, 'It's all in a good cause.'

When Lol really *was* a tiny captivating elf she would be glad that Jo had written her poem.

12

'Jo, I really *cannot* have this! You've hardly eaten a thing
– and don't tell me it's because you don't like the food! I
made this meal specially for you.'

'That's why it's muck,' said Tom. 'Soya mince – *spew*!'

'There's nothing wrong with soya mince,' said Mrs
Jameson.

'And what is more, I'll thank you to watch your
manners, young man!' That was Mr Jameson, weighing
in. Jo looked down uncomfortably at her plate, with its
helping of shepherd's pie neatly banked on one side.
'What's her problem? Why isn't she eating?'

Jo's mum hunched a shoulder and shook her head in
helpless fashion, as if to say, *don't ask me*.

'Well?' Her dad addressed her directly, forcing Jo to
look up. 'What's the matter with that dinner?'

'I just can't manage it all,' said Jo.

'Why not? I suppose you've been stuffing yourself
with junk food all day!'

She hadn't been stuffing herself with junk food – she
was making a determined effort to stick to her pact with
Lol and not to *eat* junk food. But it was Saturday and it
had poured with rain since early morning and all she'd
done was just sit about indoors, catching up on her
homework, watching television, quarrelling with Tom.
How could she be expected to consume vast mounds of

shepherd's pie and carrots when she hadn't done anything to use up any energy? Some people, it seemed to
Jo, didn't understand the *principles* of eating.

'What did she have at lunch time?'

'Banana sandwich,' said Jo. 'And an apple.'

'That's not nearly enough for a growing girl! You can't
exist on banana sandwiches and apples!'

'As a matter of fact,' said Jo, 'you probably could.
You could probably exist *very well* on –'

'Not in this house!' Her dad spoke with what Andy
called his 'heavy father' voice: it always spelt trouble. 'In
this house you'll eat what's put before you. Your mother
has enough to do without having to cope with you and
your fads. You've been pandered to for quite long
enough.'

Tom, across the table, sent her a look of malicious
triumph: it was exactly what he had said all along.

'You just get that down you,' said Mr Jameson, 'and
hurry up about it. Some of us want to get on with our
pudding.'

Jo turned in appeal to her mother. 'I can't!' she said.
'I'll be sick.'

'Jo, please!' said Mrs Jameson. 'Just try a little.'

'I've already *tried* a little. I've already eaten over half
of it.'

'Just a few more mouthfuls . . . for my sake! Please!'

'Don't waste your time pleading with her! That's the
mistake you've made all along. She's been given far too
much leeway; she's just taking advantage. You can sit
there,' said Mr Jameson, 'until you've got that down
you. I don't care if it takes the rest of the evening, you're
not moving from this table until I see an empty plate. It's

123

become ridiculous! All I ever hear is *Jo won't eat this, Jo won't eat that* . . . well, in future you can just learn to eat what the rest of us eat and stop being so fussy!'

Jo bent her head mutinously over her plate. They couldn't *force* you to eat. Not unless they did what they did to the poor suffragettes, in prison, and put tubes down you. Her dad couldn't put a tube down her because he hadn't got one. Only the inner tubes from Tom's bike and he could hardly use them.

Mrs Jameson went through to the kitchen to fetch pudding. It was cheesecake. That was all right, Jo didn't like cheesecake. Tom could rub his tummy and say 'Yum yum!' as much as he liked, it didn't bother her.

The atmosphere round the table was strained. Her dad ate in grim silence; her mum, she could feel, was unhappy – Mrs Jameson hated rows and unpleasantness. Tom concentrated on making a pig of himself, smacking his lips and spraying bits of cheesecake round the table as he talked. Andy, who might have been on Jo's side, was round at a friend's.

Jo was isolated, but stubborn. She *couldn't* eat any more. People ate far too much, all the articles you read in magazines telling you how to stay healthy said that most people in the Western world could cut their diets practically in half. It was obscene, sitting round a table gluttonising on cheesecake while people in Ethiopia and places were starving.

If her dad hadn't been there she would have said so, but Mr Jameson could get really grumpy when he was in one of his moods.

At the end of the meal Jo's dad said he was going to go and make some coffee and 'I want to see that plate cleared by the time I get back.'

124

'Jo, do try!' begged Mrs Jameson. 'We don't want trouble, do we?'

Jo poked distastefully, with her fork. 'It's not fair forcing people to eat when they don't want to!'

'Just try a little . . . just to make me happy.'

It was difficult to resist an appeal from her mother. Mrs Jameson really hated it when there were upsets in the family. Reluctantly, Jo was about to shove a forkful into her mouth (perhaps if she closed her eyes and swallowed it straight down without chewing it wouldn't be so bad) when her dad came back. He took one look at Jo's plate and said, 'Right! that's it. You've had your chance. The rest of us are going to watch television: you can stay here.' Jo, in outrage, slapped her fork back down on to her plate. 'Tom, Marjorie,' said her dad. 'Come on!'

'*Dockside Beat*!' yelled Tom, hurtling himself like a rocket down to the far end of the room where the television was kept.

Mrs Jameson, with a last appealing glance at Jo, followed him.

'When you've eaten your food,' said Jo's dad, 'you may come and join us. Not before.'

The double doors that divided the room into two were pulled shut, leaving Jo by herself in front of a plate of fast congealing shepherd's pie. She pushed it away in disgust. Nothing would make her eat it now. Not even if her dad came and *stood* over her. Not if he threatened to pull out her fingernails with red hot pincers. The suffragettes hadn't eaten and neither would she.

She tiptoed across the room and put her ear to the crack between the doors. She could just make out the theme tune for *Dockside Beat*. It was one of her favourite programmes, it had a cop who looked like a grown-up version of Robbie. But she didn't care! Not even for *Dockside Beat* was she going to allow herself to be bullied.

She went back to the table and seated herself again straight-backed, arms folded, before the shepherd's pie; a martyr to her cause.

At nine o'clock (she could just hear the fade-out music for *Dockside Beat* coming from the television) the front door opened. It was Andy, returning from his friend's. Jo sat, stiff and straight, on her chair. *Let him come and see her . . . please let him come and see her . . .*

Five minutes passed by the clock on the mantelpiece – five minutes which seemed longer than the whole of the hour which had gone before – and then, relief! The double doors slid open and Andy appeared. Now it would be all right! Andy would be on her side.

Andy closed the doors behind him and came across to the table.

'Cold shepherd's pie!' he said. 'Yeeugh!'

Tears flooded Jo's eyes. 'It's foul!'

'Well, it would be,' said Andy, 'wouldn't it? Not meant to be eaten cold. I don't expect it was foul when it was first dished up.'

'No, it wasn't,' sobbed Jo, 'but I ate as much as I could and if I eat any more I'll just be sick!'

'I reckon I'd be sick,' agreed Andy, 'eating that lot.'

'Anyone would be.' Jo put up a hand and knuckled at her eyes. She had known Andy would support her.

'Perhaps we ought to go and heat it up again?'

Heat it up? Jo looked at him, suspiciously. 'What for?'

'So it'll taste better.'

'Why?' said Jo. 'Are you going to eat it?'

'Not me,' said Andy. 'You.'

The tears sprang back again. 'I can't!'

'Why can't you?'

'I don't want it! I've had enough! I'll be sick!'

Andy pursed his lips. Jo suddenly knew that he had been sent in as an ambassador, to try and talk her into eating. She would never trust him again! Never, as long as she lived!

'You know you're worrying Mum half out of her mind,' said Andy, 'don't you? She thinks you're getting anorexic.'

'Well, I'm not!' Jo scrubbed at her eyes, defiantly. She sat up stiff and straight again on her chair. 'I just don't believe in gorging myself. People eat far too much. 'It's disgusting, when there's other people starving.'

'It's not going to help the other people that are starving if you starve, too.'

'I'm not starving! I'm not even *hungry*, let alone *starving*. You can tell Dad that I'll sit here *all night* if necessary.'

In the end they let her go to bed. Nobody said anything, not even her dad. All that happened was that her mum came in, looking defeated, took her plate away and said, 'Go on, then! Get yourself off to bed.' In the circumstances, Jo didn't like to remind her that it was Saturday and that on Saturdays she was allowed to stay up; in any case she wasn't sure that she'd want to stay up if it meant sitting in the same room as her dad and feeling great waves of displeasure coming at her.

Next morning at breakfast all the family were there,

settling down to their usual Sunday fry-up – bacon, sausages (both made from poor pigs. It was so *horrible*), eggs, mushrooms, tomatoes; Tom and Andy even had fried bread. *Ugh*. Fried bread was really gruesome. When you chewed it all the fat squidged out.

Jo approached the table warily, half expecting to be faced with demands that she eat 'the same as the rest of us', but once again there was silence. Her dad asked Andy to pass the toast, Tom said 'Fried bread! Scrummy!', but apart from that no one spoke. It was as if they had decided to call a temporary truce while they waited to see what Jo did next.

After breakfast, as usual, Lol called round. Matty and Jool didn't come any more. Now that Jo had gone all self-righteous and wouldn't let them hide in the wardrobe, they said it wasn't any fun.

At the ritual weigh-in, Jo found she had lost another half pound: Lol had managed one. It wasn't very much, but at least it was a step in the right direction.

Lol said solemnly, 'The spare tyre is starting to deflate . . .' And then she giggled and waved her fingers in Jo's face. 'Bulbous blobs!' she said. 'I've done a picture of them . . . for the poem. D'you want to see?'

Lol really wasn't so bad. At least she could laugh at herself (a little bit). It was more than Barge could do.

As they left the bathroom they tripped over Tom.

'What are you doing?' demanded Jo, automatically suspicious.

'Trying to get in!'

'Well, why didn't you *knock*?'

'I did knock, you didn't hear me . . . you were too busy weighing yourselves!' shouted Tom, as Jo and Lol disappeared into Jo's bedroom.

Dinner on Sundays was always roast. Today it was roast lamb, roast potatoes, roast parsnip and sprouts. Jo didn't terribly like roast things, and she positively *loathed* roast parsnips, but she could see from the glance her father threw at her – sharp, and warning – that there would be trouble if she didn't make an effort.

'Jo?' Her mother, over-bright, hacked off a slice of lamb and placed it on Jo's plate. Jo recoiled, in horror.

'I don't ea –'

She stopped. 'You will eat,' said Mr Jameson, 'what is put before you. Yesterday we suffered soya mince on your behalf: today you will suffer roast lamb on ours. Right? Right. I don't want to hear another word.'

There was a silence.

'Sprouts?' said Mrs Jameson. 'Tom?'

'Yes,' said Tom.

'Yes, *please*,' said Mrs Jameson.

'Yes, please,' said Tom.

'Jo?'

Jo nodded, miserably.

'Jo and the Lollipop,' said Tom, pushing a sprout into his mouth, 'were *weighing* themselves. This morning. Upstairs in the bathroom. They were there for *hours*.'

'Wow!' Andy pulled a face at Jo across the table. 'That sounds subversive! And what was old Peeping Thomas doing? Bending down with his eye to the keyhole?'

'He was spying,' said Jo.

'I was not!'

129

'So how do you know we were weighing ourselves?'

''Cause I heard you, jumping up and down off the scales!'

'Ha!' said Andy. '*Ear* to the keyhole!'

'I didn't have to put my ear to the keyhole, I could hear it just standing there . . . I could hear the scales groan as old Fa – I mean, the Lollipop climbed on them. She must have weighed herself about a dozen times.'

'So why shouldn't people weigh themselves?' Calmly Mrs Jameson piled sprouts on to Jo's plate. 'That's what scales are there for, for people to weigh themselves!'

Tom scowled: he had been hoping to get Jo into trouble. 'Not to keep *on* doing it,' he said.

'We didn't keep on doing it! We did it *once*.'

'And how much do you weigh?' asked Mrs Jameson, trying to make it sound like just a casual question.

'Can't remember,' said Jo.

'You've got a mighty short memory!' That was her dad, suddenly coming to life. 'I was under the impression this only took place a couple of hours ago?'

'Well – but it was Lol, really. She's trying to –' Jo broke off, biting her tongue. She had given her faithful promise not to tell a soul.

'Trying to what?' said Mrs Jameson.

'She was just interested,' said Jo, 'in knowing what she weighs . . . she wanted to check our scales against hers, because she thinks hers might be wrong.'

'Most likely she got on hers and they gave way,' said Tom. He ducked as his mother's hand came whipping across the table. 'Bathroom scales aren't meant for weighing elephants!'

One thing you could say for Tom, he really was quite

unsquashable. In the commotion which followed –
'Tom, if I have to tell you again –' 'I didn't *say* anything!
What did I say? I didn't *say* anything!' – Jo hoped she
might be able to get away with just pushing her food
round her plate and mashing it to look as though she had
eaten some, but she was aware all the time of her dad's
eye upon her. She didn't want another row like last
night. Bit by bit she forced it down her. She couldn't
make up her mind which was the less painful, chewing it
until it was a horrid pulpy mess going round and round
her mouth or swallowing it straight down so that it felt
like lead dumplings plopping into her stomach.

'Good girl!' Her mother took her plate away. She
sounded really pleased; relieved, too. 'That wasn't so
bad, was it?'

Jo managed a smile, though rather a trembly one. All
the sprouts and potatoes and loathsome parsnip were
swimming around in her stomach in the most disgusting
fashion, all mixed up with meat fat and *blood*. It was
making her feel sick.

'And now for pudding . . . one of your favourites!'

Mrs Jameson bore it through in triumph from the
kitchen. She placed it on the table, in front of Jo: lemon
meringue pie. Jo swallowed. The pie sat there before
her, glistening and gleaming like a pile of dog sick.

'Big slice or little slice?' Mrs Jameson stood poised,
ready to cut into the yucky yellow goo.

Jo just managed to say 'little slice' before a wodge of
undigested *something* rose into her mouth and almost
choked her.

'Little slice, *please*,' said her dad.

'Little slice, *please*,' said Jo.

Her mum had obviously done the pie specially for her; she couldn't not eat it. She reminded herself that normally she *liked* lemon meringue. (But then normally she wasn't forced to eat things which made her feel sick. Her father was *evil*, making her eat meat.)

'There we are!' said Jo's mum.

Glup! went Jo, bravely, *Glob*, went the pie. Slosh, went the contents of her stomach.

'You see?' Her dad nodded at her, approvingly 'It's only a question of mind over matter.'

13

One Thursday, in gym, Jo fell off the parallel bars. She had never done such a thing in her life before. She had slipped occasionally, just like anyone else – even Nadge had been known to slip *occasionally* – but she had never actually fallen right off. She still couldn't work out how it had happened. One minute she had been standing there, perfectly balanced (and feeling pleasantly superior to Barge and Gerry Stubbs, perilously wobbling on either side of her), the next minute she had found herself crashing floorwards. It was really rather scary.

'I say, are you all right?' Barge's big square face was peering down at her, from the bars. 'You've gone quite green!'

'You'd better hadn't move,' counselled Gerry. 'You might have broken something.'

'Yes, like your back or something.' Barge landed on the floor beside her with a thud. 'If people break their backs they can't ever walk again.'

Jo didn't *think* she had broken her back, though she felt somewhat bruised and shaken. She sat up, carefully.

'Keep still!' roared Barge, sending her plummeting backwards again with a karate blow to the chest. 'Moving could be *fatal*!'

'Jo?' That was Miss Daley hurrying over. She sounded concerned but just a tiny bit impatient. Miss Daley had no sympathy with people who were clumsy and inept, especially when they were members of her special gym team. You expected people like Barge to go falling over and hurt themselves: you didn't expect members of the special gym team to do so. Not, at least, when they were in an ordinary everyday gym class doing exercises that a five-year-old could have tackled.

'What happened?'

'She just *fell*,' said Barge.

'Quite suddenly,' said Gerry.

'Without any warning.'

'Just plummeted.'

'*Bang*.'

Miss Daley frowned as she bent over Jo, feeling for broken bones, 'What were you doing?'

'I wasn't doing anything,' said Jo. 'Just sort of . . . standing.'

'She was,' agreed Barge. 'She was just standing.'

'And then she plummeted –'

'*Bang*.'

'Out of nowhere.'

'There was nothing we could have done,' said Barge.

'Absolutely nothing.'

Gerry, too, was now hovering, as were the rest of the class. Miss Daley waved them aside, irritably.

'Don't all crowd round like a load of silly sheep! Move back and give us some air. Jo, I don't think there's anything actually broken. Can you manage to stand?'

Jo scrambled with alacrity to her feet. There wasn't anything *wrong* with her.

'You'd better come alone to the Office and sit down for a while. The rest of you, go and get changed and take an early break.'

'I'm perfectly OK,' said Jo. 'Honestly!'

'Be that as it may –' firmly Miss Daley shepherded her across the gym and out through the swing doors – 'you are coming with me to the Office. What did you have for breakfast this morning?'

'A banana,' said Jo. 'And an orange.'

'A banana and an orange? Doesn't your mother make toast or porridge?'

'Yes,' said Jo. But toast and porridge were fattening; at least they were if you had marmalade and sugar with them. Toast with just marge was really foul, and porridge without sugar tasted like warmed-up snot, and anyway she had made the Lollipop sign a pact that she would eat only fresh fruit for breakfast. She had made her do it last Sunday, when the Lollipop had clambered on the scales and hadn't lost a single ounce since the Sunday before. Since she claimed 'hardly ever' to eat any tea or supper, and since Jo had seen what she ate in the school canteen, they had come to the conclusion that it must be the breakfast toast-and-honey that was doing it. (She had already, at Jo's insistence, given up bacon and eggs.)

'So if your mother cooks proper food,' said Miss Daley, piloting Jo along the corridor, 'why don't you eat it?'

'I don't feel like it at that time in the morning.'

'Well, you'd better start feeling like it! If you want to continue being part of the special gym team . . .'

Jo looked up, horrified. Was Miss Daley *threatening* her?

'The fact is,' said Miss Daley, 'you need to be strong to be a gymnast . . . you need *muscles*. You need *stamina*.

135

You won't get that by starving yourself. Look at you!' She closed her fingers round Jo's arm. 'You're all skin and bone!'

Jo resented that. No one ever said that Claire was all skin and bone. They said that Claire was slim, or tiny (or petite if they wanted to show off). Slim and tiny were flattering: skin and bone meant you looked all pinched and wizened. *Did* she look all pinched and wizened?

She shot an anxious glance at herself in the full-length mirror in the Office, while Miss Daley explained what had happened. Her face stared back at her. It looked, disappointingly, exactly the same as it had always looked: round and chubby, like a squirrel with a mouthful of nuts. All that dieting hadn't done a *thing*. You'd have thought at least she'd have developed some interesting hollows or some cheekbones.

'You'd better come and sit down,' said Miss Daley, 'and stay here till break is over. I'll send someone along with a bun and a glass of milk for you.'

'Oh, but I d –' began Jo. She faltered into silence as Miss Daley, without saying anything, raised both eyebrows into her hair line. Miss Daley could have quelled a whole riot of soccer hooligans with her eyebrows. She was not a person to be argued with. When the milk came, brought to her by Fij, Jo didn't dare not to drink it.

'And the bun,' said Fij.

Jo looked at her, beseechingly. Fij *knew* she didn't like school buns, with the nasty squidgy currants and bits of peel. Fij very sternly shook her head.

'Miss Daley said I was to make sure.'

'I shall be sick,' warned Jo. Already she could feel the

136

horrible yucky milk churning and curdling in her stomach. She *never* drank cows' milk. Cows' milk was meant for calves, not for human beings. It would all come out with a great big splodge, all over the floor, along with bits of bun and half-chewed currant. Then Fij would be sorry.

'Miss Daley said to tell you,' said Fij, 'that you're not to go to special gym class tonight.'

'But that's not fair!' wailed Jo. 'I'm all right now!'

Fij shrugged. 'She said she'll talk to you next week. You can understand it, really,' said Fij. 'She doesn't want people passing out on her and breaking their necks every five seconds.'

'I didn't pass out!'

'You did almost. I was watching you. You sort of . . . *swayed*,' said Fij, hypnotically wafting herself to and fro. 'It's what happens when people don't eat enough.'

'I do eat enough!' Jo ate enough: other people ate too much.

'Last year in the Homestead,' said Fij, for all the world as if Jo had never spoken, 'we had this girl called Pria who used to faint every morning in assembly. They discovered in the end it was because she wasn't eating any breakfast.'

'*I'm* eating breakfast!'

'Yes, but you're not eating lunch, hardly. I told Miss Daley,' said Fij, 'that I'd keep an eye on you.'

Jo was outraged. 'You never!'

'I did. She asked me. She said, "You're a friend of Jo's, aren't you, Felicity? I'd like you to keep an eye on her for me".'

'That's spying!' cried Jo.

137

'No, it's not. It would only be spying if you didn't know about it. But you do know, 'cause I've told you. And anyway,' said Fij, 'it's for your own good.'

Jo didn't know what to do when it came to lunch time. Fij was there, shadowing her every move, buzzing away at her elbow like a great hover fly, with Barge and Bozzy bringing up the rear, hemming her in so there was no way of escape. They kept pointing at things they thought she should eat – 'Pie –', '*Pizza* –', 'Fish and chips!'

Jo wouldn't actually have minded a plate of fish and chips, just so long as it wasn't fishy sort of fish. (She only liked fish that didn't taste of fish, like cod or sometimes haddock. She couldn't stand plaice, all wet and slippy.)

'Go on!' said Fij. 'Have some!'

Jo was tempted. She hadn't had chips for ages, and they were all brown and crinkly, just the way she liked them. If they'd been great fat white slugs it would have been different. But brown and crinkly . . .

'You know,' said Barge, heartily, 'that eating is really terribly simple. All you have to do is open your mouth and put something inside and chew for a bit and then swallow. Anyone can do it, practically. Anyone that's not a new-born baby, that is.'

'Or anyone that's not old and toothless,' said Bozzy.

'Even someone that's old and toothless can suck and chumble.'

'Well, and even new-born babies can *gum*.'

They looked at Jo, challengingly. At that moment Lol walked past, proudly carrying a tray with yoghurt and fruit juice and a small blob of risotto. Jo *couldn't* eat fish and chips in front of Lol; it would be a gross betrayal.

On the other hand she had to eat something so that Fij

could report back to Miss Daley. She couldn't bear it if Miss Daley were to throw her out of the special gym team.

'Just a tiny ickle chippy wippy?' pleaded Fij, resorting to baby talk. She held one out, pushing it at Jo's mouth. Jo pressed her lips resolutely together.

'I'll have some risotto,' she said.

'Well, risotto is better than nothing.'

'Especially with lashings of tomato sauce,' said Bozzy.

'But only a *little* bit . . . not a whopping great plateful.'

'Nobody gets whopping great platefuls in this establishment. Lucky if you get enough to keep a *flea* alive. But if there's anything you really can't manage,' said Bozzy, 'I daresay I might be able to give you a hand.'

'Or a mouth.' said Barge, 'as the case may be.'

'She's not going to *need* a mouth,' said Fij, 'because she's going to finish it all by herself . . . *aren't* you?'

With Fij watching her like a hawk and Miss Daley parading the canteen and casting the odd sharp glance in her direction, Jo meekly did as she was told.

'There's a good girl!' crooned Fij, sounding just like Jo's mum.

Barge leaned across and patted her on the head. (A pat from Barge was like being swiped with a ten-ton fly swatter.)

'Diddums eatums lunchums 'en?'

'She ate the *lot*,' marvelled Bozzy, pulling Jo's plate towards her and somewhat desolately surveying its emptiness.

'You see it was quite easy really, wasn't it?' crooned Barge. 'Open, fill, chew, swallow . . . that's all you've got to remember.'

Later that afternoon, when Barge and Co. were safely out of the way, Lol come up and hissed, 'I had grapefruit for breakfast . . . *without sugar*! Tonight I'm going to have just plain salad, with special low-calorie dressing.'

Tonight, thought Jo, she would make up for it. Tonight she would have nothing at all – or perhaps just the teeniest tiniest dab.

She beamed, encouragingly, at Lol. 'You're doing really well,' she said.

That night, for tea, Mrs Jameson had prepared vegetable cutlets and creamy mashed potatoes with HP sauce. Jo adored mashed potatoes and HP sauce.

'Jo?' said her mother.

'Yes, please,' said Jo.

She said it before she could stop herself, and spent the rest of the evening racked with terrible guilt.

On Saturday it was Mr Jameson's birthday and they were all going out for a meal to celebrate.

'Where would you like to eat?'

Tom clamoured for McDonald's, Andy wanted Chinese.

'Jo?' said her mother. 'Where would you like?'

'Don't ask her!' yelled Tom. 'She never eats anything anyway!'

'She will tonight,' said Mr Jameson. 'Tonight's my birthday.'

The restaurant, in the end, was chosen by Jo's mum – she wanted to go back to Alberto's, which was where she had gone on the night of her wedding anniversary. Alberto's was the restaurant that was owned by Mr

Bustamente. Jo prayed there would be something on the menu she could eat.

She tugged anxiously at her mother's sleeve as they got out of the car.

'Suppose there's nothing I like?'

'Don't worry,' said Mrs Jameson. 'There's bound to be something . . . risotto – spaghetti – you like spaghetti! Spaghetti with tomato sauce, French fries –'

But they're all *fattening*, thought Jo. How could she sit and eat spaghetti and French fries in Lol's dad's restaurant when she had made Lol promise, and swear on her honour, not to touch them?

The first thing they saw as they walked through the door was Lol herself, cosily sitting at a table at the far end with a woman who must be her mother. You could tell she was Lol's mother because she looked exactly like an older fatter version of Lol.

'There's Laurel and Mrs Bustamente,' said Jo's mum. 'Let's just go and say hallo.'

Jo trailed down the restaurant after her mother. As Lol looked up and saw them, a tidal wave of scarlet washed across her face. Quickly she snatched up a menu and pulled it in front of her plate, pretending to study it. Not quickly enough. Jo had seen – and could hardly believe it! LOL'S PLATE WAS PILED HIGH WITH SPAGHETTI. As if that weren't enough, she had a second plate containing French fries. *And* a glass of what looked suspiciously like milkshake.

Jo's eyes met Lol's over the top of the menu. Lol said nothing. There wasn't much she could say, though her eyes pleaded with Jo to be merciful.

Jo wasn't feeling merciful. What she was feeling was

murderous. She turned and stalked back up the restaurant. Already Tom was greedily consulting the menu, reading it out loud as he tried to decide between a king-size pizza with all the toppings or a king-size burger with a double helping of French fries.

'Jo?' said her dad. 'What about you?'

'I'm going to have spaghetti and chips,' said Jo, 'with lashings of tomato sauce, and a glass of Coke, and a banana split to follow and I'll have garlic bread to start with.'

There was a silence.

'Are you being funny?' said Mr Jameson.

'No,' said Jo. 'I'm *hungry*.'

Her mother had come back to the table. 'Poor Laurel!' She shook her head as she sat down next to Mr Jameson. 'You can see why it's so difficult for her to lose weight.'

Tom stared fixedly at Jo. 'I know someone else who's going to look like that if she's not careful.'

Jo picked up the menu. 'I think I might have an ice-cream as well.'

She felt sick afterwards, and she didn't care; not one, single, tiny little bit! And she didn't bother to weigh herself, either.

14

First thing on Saturday morning the Lollipop rang.

'I just wanted to explain,' she said, 'about last night.'

Jo didn't see what there was to explain. Lol had been caught in the act of gluttony, and it was no use pretending it was an isolated incident because it quite obviously *wasn't*.

'It's the first time I've had a meal at the restaurant for ages,' babbled Lol. 'Ages and *ages*. Not since before I went on holiday, almost.'

Even if it were – and Jo wasn't at all sure that she believed it – that was still no excuse for stuffing herself with spaghetti and chips, not to mention a great gluggy milkshake.

'Truly!' squeaked Lol.

Jo twisted the telephone cord round her fingers. She didn't like to say straight out that she thought Lol was lying. On the other hand she couldn't bring herself to say 'That's all right, just so long as it doesn't happen again' because it almost certainly would happen again. It had been happening all along, right from the beginning: Lol had been *cheating*. Cheating all the time. It was why she'd never been able to lose any weight. Jo had known there had to be a reason.

'I hope you don't think I've done it before,' said Lol, sounding aggrieved.

Jo made a mumbling noise into the telephone.

'Because I jolly well *haven't*!' said Lol.

There was a silence.

'You can come and ask my dad! You can ask my mum
. . . she'll tell you! I've hardly eaten a *thing* – not for
weeks and weeks! And anyway,' said Lol, suddenly
turning spiteful, 'what about all that that you ate? You
had ice-cream *and* banana split! My mum said she'd
never seen anything like it. She said it just went to show
how unfair it was . . . someone like you can eat and eat
and *eat*, and someone like me starves, practically, and
I'm the one that puts on weight and people like you just
jeer and sneer.'

'I've never jeered and sneered!' said Jo.

'Yes, you have! You said I was too fat to play Posy.'

'Well, you are too fat to play Posy! And last night was
the first time I've had chips in *weeks*, and you know that
that's true 'cause you've seen the evidence!'

'But it's the first time I've had them,' wailed Lol.

'In that case there must be something wrong with you!
You ought to go and see a doctor . . . get your glands
tested, or something. I'm just about sick of it!'

Jo slammed down the receiver. Her whole body was
trembling; she really didn't like having rows and shouting at people. Barge and Bozzy might thrive on it, but it
upset Jo.

She turned to rush upstairs, only to bump headlong
into her mother on her way down. Mrs Jameson must
have heard everything she'd said. Jo braced herself for a
lecture. (*How many times have I told you? Be nice to
Laurel!*)

'Jo?' Mrs Jameson put out a hand, to steady her.

'What's the matter? Was that Laurel? Have you had words?'

'She's been cheating!' cried Jo. It burst out of her before she could stop it. 'She's been eating all these gruesome things and then she thinks it's my fault if she's still fat . . . I can't watch over her twenty-four hours of the day!'

'Of course you can't!' Mrs Jameson's voice was brisk and sympathetic. 'Nor should you have to. I'm sure you've done your best – in fact, I know you have!' She gave Jo a quick hug. 'But enough is enough. Yes?' Jo nodded. 'You can't fight other people's battles for them, Joey. You've done everything you can; from now on it has to be up to Laurel. All I'd say is, try not to be *too* cross . . . it really isn't easy for her.'

'If she comes on Sunday,' quavered Jo, 'will you tell her that I'm out?'

'We'll see,' said Mrs Jameson. 'Maybe she won't come.'

'Well, but if she *does* –'

Fortunately, Lol didn't. Even she, it seemed, had finally got the message. Jo went next door to Matty's, and from Matty's they went round to Jool's.

'Don't tell me,' said Jool, 'that you finally managed to get rid of her?'

Jo flushed. It sounded horribly callous, put like that.

'What happened? Did you tell her to push off?'

'N-not exactly –' She'd just said she was sick of her; though she supposed, in the end, that that was just as bad.

'I told you,' said Jool. 'I told you you'd have to be brutal.'

* * *

On Monday morning Jo did her best to avoid the Lollipop, which was quite easy as the Lollipop was obviously doing her best to avoid Jo. She had taken, just recently, to going round with a stick-like girl from Roper's called Neelum Rajah. Jo overheard her in the playground at break: Lol was describing the time she had flown on Concorde, and Neelum was listening politely with every show of interest. Maybe she really was interested. Jo hoped so.

On Tuesday after English, Gerry Stubbs came round the class with a large brown envelope demanding magazine contributions. Jo wished, now, that she had persisted with her poem about the dinosaur. In the circumstances, the Before-and-After one seemed a bit sick, but it was too late to do anything about it at this stage. She couldn't *not* make a contribution; Barge & Co. would never let her hear the end of it. (It would come under the heading of 'Letting the House down'.)

'Jam?' That was Gerry, holding out her brown envelope. Jo took her folder from her bag and carefully extracted a copy of Before-and-After.

'Here you are.'

'What is it?' Gerry peered at it. 'Oh! A poem. How original! Everyone in the whole class,' she said, 'seems to have done poems except me.'

Yes, thought Jo, but mine is a *good* poem. She knew it was a good poem. It was the best poem she had ever written.

'Was that your dinosaur one? demanded Barge, leaning across Claire to address Jo.

'Er – no,' said Jo. 'That was another one.'

'So what happened to the dinosaur one?'

'It sort of . . . *languished*,' said Jo. 'If you know what I mean?'

'You mean it didn't get anywhere,' said Fij, trying to be helpful.

'Well, yes . . . I suppose that is one way of putting it.'

'So what is this one about?'

'Oh! Something quite different. You'll see,' said Jo, quickly, 'when it's published.'

'I beg your pardon?' Barge, still leaning across Claire as if she were a bit of old furniture, cupped an astonished hand to her ear. 'Did I hear you say *when*?'

Jo blushed. 'I mean, of course, *if* . . . *if* it's published.'

'Hm!' Barge looked at Jo out of narrowed eyes. There were still occasions when she and Bozzy felt it necessary to remind her of the fact that they were ex-Homsteaders and she a mere New Girl. 'It is not every one,' said Barge, grandly, 'who has the gift of writing poetry. There are those of us who can, and those of us who can't. I wouldn't wish to depress you,' said Barge, 'but you must be prepared for disappointment.'

'Oh, I am,' grovelled Jo. 'I am! All I meant was that it would have seemed a bit pushy to have come up to you and said "Look at what I've written" *before* it was published – *if* it's published – because, I mean, you mightn't have *wanted* to look at it, you might have found it quite incredibly boring, or incredibly inconvenient, or incredibly – well! Incredibly almost anything,' said Jo. 'So that's why I thought I'd wait until it's published – *if* it's published. Because I didn't want you to be incredibly bored and feel you had to pretend to be interested when you most likely weren't.'

147

'Well, that is understandable,' said Barge, mollified. 'Though you could always have come and said "Please give me your honest opinion and tell me where I have gone wrong" . . . we should have been only too happy,' said Barge, magnanimously, 'to oblige.'

'I didn't think of that,' said Jo, crestfallen.

'Never mind.' Barge was all affability now that she had successfully squashed any pretensions. 'We live and we learn.'

'Yes,' agreed Jo, humbly.

'You'll know better next time.' Barge sat back complacently on her chair, almost knocking Claire's head off on the way. 'Just because this year's contribution will most probably be returned with a rejection slip you mustn't be put off trying again.'

'Oh, I *won't* be,' said Jo. 'Not now I know.'

Inside herself she was thinking that it was really very easy to handle people like Barge: you just had to agree with everything they said and then go away and do your own thing. She couldn't imagine why Bozzy seemed to find it so difficult. In spite of being best friends, she and Barge were forever fighting, threatening to kneecap each other or push each other's teeth down their throats. Jo and Fij hardly fought at all.

That lunch time, in the canteen, Lol passed Jo with her tray piled high. She didn't look in Jo's direction, she was too busy talking to Neelum Rajah, meekly trotting at her side with a plate of salad and a glass of water.

'Some people,' Lol was saying, 'are just *made* big.'

Some people, thought Jo, sadly, just made themselves big. She couldn't be cross any more, though she still had lingering regrets. She knew her mum was right, you

148

couldn't fight other people's battles for them, but it would have given her a sense of achievement to see Lol looking like an elf. And in an odd sort of way she was going to miss their Sunday morning sessions together. She wondered what Lol had done with the *Count Your Calories* book. Left it on a bus, probably.

One day during the last week of term, Gerry Stubbs's big brown envelope came winging its way back from the Magazine Committee. Inside it were all the entries which they had decided not to use, with duplicated slips attached to each one saying: *The Magazine Committee thanks you for your contribution but regrets they are unable to make use of it on this occasion.*

Barge was almost apoplectic: not only her and Fij's efforts had been returned, but so had Bozzy's – in spite of being written in Latin. Barge seemed to take it as almost a personal insult.

'Just listen to this, everyone!' She snatched the copy of Bozzy's poem and waved it aloft to attract people's attention. 'Just *listen* . . . *Caesar adsum jam for tea, Pinny aderat* . . . CAESAR – and PINNY! Two of the greatest names in all Latin! Why, there probably wouldn't *be* any Latin, hardly, without Caesar and Pinny! And all they can say is, *we thank you for your contribution* . . . huh!' Barge tossed the sheet of paper contemptuously in the air. 'Load of morons!'

There was a silence as the paper floated slowly to earth.

'It's Pliny, actually,' said Pru Frank. 'Not Pinny.'

'As if it makes any difference!' Barge huffed, scornfully. 'What do you know about it, anyway?'

'I've seen it before. The poem, I mean . . . *Caesar adsum jam for tea. Pliny aderat* . . . it's quite well known,' said Pru.

'Ho, is it?' snorted Barge. 'Some people,' she confided in a loud voice to Jo, 'will say anything to try and get in on the act.'

'Oh, quite,' agreed Jo; though she noticed that Bozzy had nipped out of the room pretty smartish. 'I expect what it was,' she said comfortingly, 'I expect it was simply too highbrow for them.'

It wasn't till later in the day, when Barge had accused Bozzy of bringing shame on them by blatantly copying the poem out of a book and Bozzy had brazenly said 'So what?' and the whole thing had degenerated into one of their slanging matches – 'I'll rip your guts out!' 'I'll spiflicate your eyeballs!' – that Fij suddenly said, 'What about Jammy? I didn't see her get a rejection slip.'

Hostilities ceased, abruptly.

'*Did* you? said Barge.

'Um – no,' admitted Jo. What Jo had got was a note saying: *The Magazine Committee thank you for your contribution which they are pleased to accept for publication*.

'Well!' said Bozzy.

'Obviously a fluke,' said Barge.

'Or beginner's luck.'

'*Or* beginner's luck,' Barge repeated.

'We haven't even *seen* it,' said Fij.

'Do you want to?' Jo didn't mind, now that she knew it was going to be published. She took a copy from her folder and passed it over. The three of them read it, slowly and in frowning silence.

150

'It's good,' said Fij, at last.

'Yes, it is,' said Bozzy.

'It's very good.'

'Yes, it is. It's *very* good.'

'Not bad at all,' agreed Barge. Graciously she handed it back. 'Just so long as you don't let it go to your head . . . you mustn't expect it to happen every time, you know.'

'Oh, I wouldn't,' said Jo.

'But for a beginner you are to be congratulated. Very promising,' said Barge. 'There's only one thing that bothers me about it –'

'What's that?'

'Well, people are bound to think it's about the Lollipop, seeing as she's done the illustrations – which I suppose,' said Barge, grudgingly, 'are better than I could have done. But the thing is, it's quite obviously *not* about the Lollipop. I mean, not unless it's fantasy time.'

Bozzy giggled. '*I look in the mirror and what do I see? A lump of fat! Can it be me*?'

'Don't be rotten,' said Jo. She put the poem back in the folder. 'She did try. And it's not her fault . . . some people,' said Jo, 'are just *made* big.'

Other great reads from **Red Fox**

Further Red Fox titles that you might enjoy reading are listed on the following pages. They are available in bookshops or they can be ordered directly from us.

If you would like to order books, please send this form and the money due to:

ARROW BOOKS, BOOKSERVICE BY POST, PO BOX 29, DOUGLAS, ISLE OF MAN, BRITISH ISLES. Please enclose a cheque or postal order made out to Arrow Books Ltd for the amount due, plus 30p per book for postage and packing to a maximum of £3.00, both for orders within the UK. For customers outside the UK, please allow 35p per book.

NAME _____

ADDRESS _____

_____

Please print clearly.

Whilst every effort is made to keep prices low, it is sometimes necessary to increase cover prices at short notice. If you are ordering books by post, to save delay it is advisable to phone to confirm the correct price. The number to ring is THE SALES DEPARTMENT 071 (if outside London) 973 9700.

Other great reads from **Red Fox**

The Maggie Series   Joan Lingard

MAGGIE 1: THE CLEARANCE

Sixteen-year-old Maggie McKinley's dreading the prospect of a whole summer with her granny in a remote Scottish glen. But the holiday begins to look more exciting when Maggie meets the Frasers. She soon becomes best friends with James and spends almost all her time with him. Which leads, indirectly, to a terrible accident . . .

ISBN 0 09 947730 0   £1.99

MAGGIE 2: THE RESETTLING

Maggie McKinley's family has been forced to move to a high rise flat and her mother is on the verge of a nervous breakdown. As her family begins to rely more heavily on her, Maggie finds less and less time for her schoolwork and her boyfriend James. The pressures mount and Maggie slowly realizes that she alone must control the direction of her life.

ISBN 0 09 949220 2   £1.99

MAGGIE 3: THE PILGRIMAGE

Maggie is now seventeen. Though a Glaswegian through and through, she is very much looking forward to a cycling holiday with her boyfriend James. But James begins to annoy Maggie and tensions mount. Then they meet two Canadian boys and Maggie finds she is strongly attracted to one of them.

ISBN 0 09 951190 8   £2.50

MAGGIE 4: THE REUNION

At eighteen, Maggie McKinley has been accepted for university and is preparing to face the world. On her first trip abroad, she flies to Canada to a summer au pair job and a reunion with Phil, the Canadian student she met the previous summer. But as usual in Maggie's life, events don't go quite as planned . . .

ISBN 0 09 951260 2   £2.50

Other great reads *from* **Red Fox**

THE WINTER VISITOR   Joan Lingard

Strangers didn't come to Nick Murray's home town in winter.
And they didn't lodge at his house. But Ed Black had—and Nick
Murray didn't like it.

Why had Ed come? The small Scottish seaside resort was
bleak, cold and grey at that time of year. The answer, Nick
begins to suspect, lies with his mother—was there some past
connection between her and Ed?

ISBN 0 09 938590 2   £1.99

STRANGERS IN THE HOUSE   Joan Lingard

Calum resents his mother remarrying. He doesn't want to move
to a flat in Edinburgh with a new father and a thirteen-year-old
stepsister. Stella, too, dreads the new marriage. Used to living
alone with her father she loathes the idea of sharing their small
flat.

Stella's and Calum's struggles to adapt to a new life, while
trying to cope with the problems of growing up are related with
great poignancy in a book which will be enjoyed by all older
readers.

ISBN 0 09 955020 2   £2.99